over my brother's dead body, chase andrews

piper rayne

Cover Design: By Hang Le

1st Line Editor: Joy Editing

2nd Line Editor: My Brother's Editor

Proofreader: My Brother's Editor

about over my brother's dead body, chase andrews

Chase Andrews.

The Kingsmen's top tight end.
My brother's friend and teammate.
My new neighbor.
The grumpy to my sunshine.

But underneath that grumpy exterior, there's so much more.

Chase likes to pretend nothing affects him, but I've seen glimpses of his other side in the time we've spent together.

And the more we get to know each other, the more I'm falling for him.

Under normal circumstances, this would be great. Except my hyper-protective big brother thinks no man is good enough for me, and my ex-fiancé is trying to win me back.

One charming, seemingly good man already broke my heart. Am I stupid to give a self-confessed relationship-adverse football player a chance to break it a second time?

OVER MY BROTHER'S DEAD BODY,

Chase Andrews

one

. . .

Twyla

I place the final pile of clothing into my suitcase and lay my body over it so I can zip it closed, saying a silent prayer that it doesn't come off the conveyor belt at the airport busted open with my bras and panties hanging out. That would be just my luck recently, adding misery to heartbreak since my fiancé broke off our engagement months ago because he'd fallen for someone else.

There's a knock on my door and I turn around to see my parents standing in the doorway. No doubt they're here for one last-ditch effort to convince me to stay. They don't understand that everywhere I look is a memory of what I thought my life would be.

"Well, I'm all packed. My ride should be here soon," I say, trying to convey it's no use trying to talk me out of this, I am indeed flying across the country to live in San Francisco.

"Honey, are you sure you want to do this?" My mom steps into my room, arms outstretched, and grips me by the shoulders.

I love my mom. We have a close relationship, always doing stuff together, from tending to our vegetable garden in the summer to being members of the same book club. I'm going to miss her terribly, and I wish things were different, I really do, but ever since Mathew called off the wedding, everyone in our small town looks at me with pity. I can't stand the whispers anymore. I'm trying my best to move forward, but this town is a constant reminder of what he did. If I stay here, I'll forever be the girl whose fiancé ditched her for someone else.

Enter San Francisco.

My big brother, Miles, is the safety for the San Francisco Kingsmen football team, and I've visited him numerous times over the years. I even consider some of his teammates my friends—they're certainly more than acquaintances.

I always enjoy my time there, and one day, I thought, what if? I searched the internet for living arrangements and stumbled upon a condo and pet-sitting job for some tech guy who will be away for months, and I applied on impulse. To my surprise, I got the job and took it as a sign that I should head west and get the hell out of my small town in Connecticut.

"I'm sure, Mom. It won't be forever. I just need to clear my head. I'll be back."

She gives me a small smile as though she doesn't believe me. I honestly don't know if she should. I don't plan on staying longer than my house-sitting job lasts, but the idea of returning here feels mountainous right now. Now that Mathew has broken my image of the future, I like the idea of not being anchored anywhere.

Regardless, I teach elementary school, and San Francisco is so expensive to live in I doubt I could afford to live there on a teacher's salary even if I wanted to stay. But even a few months away from everything Mathew will do me good.

"Is Miles picking you up at the airport?" my dad asks.

I concentrate on lifting my suitcase off the bed, and my dad groans.

"You still haven't told him?" His voice is full of disapproval.

"It's a surprise," I say in my bright and cheery teacher voice—the one I use when it's raining and I tell the kids recess is inside.

The truth is, I have no idea how my brother will react to me living in the same city as him. A short visit is one thing, but will I hold him back if I'm there longer?

He's the epitome of an overbearing, overprotective big brother, and I'm hoping he won't play dad to me the entire time I'm there. I might still be reeling from my breakup, but I'm an adult, and I don't need him or anyone else watching over me twenty-four seven.

"If you're talking to him, please don't tell him until I do…" I give them my best pleading eyes.

They glance at one another then back at me, nodding with reluctance.

"Just make sure you do it as soon as you're settled. I don't like the idea of you in that big city all alone." My mom frowns.

"Mom, I've been there lots of times. I know my way around."

"Sure, but I've always felt better knowing you were at your brother's place and he was watching out for you."

"I'm a grown woman. I don't need him to be my babysitter."

My dad rubs his hand down my upper arm. "We just worry about you, sweetie. Especially after what happened."

I point at him. "And that is exactly why I have to leave. So I can distance myself from what happened and be around people who don't know."

My dad's thin lips suggest he doesn't agree, but he nods anyway. "Here, I'll take your suitcase downstairs." He steps forward and lifts it. "Jeez, do you have a dead body in here?"

I roll my eyes. "Funny, funny."

He says the same thing every time he picks up a suitcase of mine.

Tears spring to my eyes. I'm going to miss my parents. As much as I want to flee from this town, I love my family. My friends jokingly call us the Cleavers—a nod to the perfect family from the 1950s sitcom *Leave it to Beaver.*

"Oh, sweetie." My mom draws me into a hug, and I wrap my arms around her. "It's okay to admit you made a mistake. If you need to come home, we'll be here."

I nod into her neck. They'd welcome me back, no questions asked, I know that. But it's time for me to leave the nest. Not just because of my failed relationship but because I'm twenty-five and I still live in my childhood home.

I need to spread my wings and discover whether I'll soar to new heights or fall flat on my face.

two

. . .

Chase

How the hell did I get roped into this bullshit?

I'm a tight end for the San Francisco Kingsmen, not fucking Martha Stewart. What do I know about hosting an engagement party?

Don't get me wrong, I'm happy for our wide receiver Brady and his former nanny, Violet. At least I don't have to listen to him groan anymore about how he lost her, because they're engaged. Great. Isn't that between the two of them, not the rest of us?

My teammates insisted I host tonight's shenanigans since I've never hosted anything but a poker game, so here we are. It's really their punishment, not mine.

Looking at the spread on my kitchen island, I could do worse. Pork rinds, bowls of chips, a veggie tray for the women, and I plan to order pizza once everyone's here. There's beer in the fridge. What more do we need?

My condo isn't enormous—three bedrooms, two baths, a big kitchen that's separate from the massive living/dining room combo—but it's bigger than the house I grew up in. That living room is the entire reason I bought it, and rather than putting in some formal dining table, I made the whole space what some might consider a man cave.

An eighty-inch flat-screen TV hangs on one wall, connected to a state-of-the-art sound system. It's across from a huge sectional, and behind that is my pool table, poker table, darts, and a few pinball machines. All the shit I enjoyed growing up in Small Town, Montana.

The first knock lands on my door, and I pull at the collar of my shirt. I've already undone the first button. I crack my neck while walking over to the door. Tonight promises to be a long night.

I open the door to a smiling Lee and Shayna. Lee's the team's quarterback, and Shayna is one of the team's athletic trainers and also Lee's fiancée. Yeah, that's two of my teammates engaged. It's almost like commitment is contagious, the way they both fell so fast.

"Hey." I manage to give them a half smile.

"I see you're already in the hosting mood." Lee chuckles and claps me on the shoulder.

"Hey, Chase. Don't worry, it won't be that bad." Shayna's trying to hold back a laugh at my obvious discomfort.

"Says you." I step back from the door and wave them in.

"Oh." Shayna comes up short and looks around the living/dining room. "I wasn't sure what to expect, but somehow this completely fits the brand."

"Brand?" I scowl.

"Grumpy introverted bachelor who plays professional football."

I shake my head.

"Go easy on him, babe. It's his first time hosting anything more than poker night, right, Chase?" Lee shrugs out of his coat and helps Shayna out of hers. "Where should we put these?" Lee holds up their coats.

"Um…" I look around, take them, and toss them on the pool table.

"Chase? How about your second bedroom?" Shayna suggests, and I want to ask her why the hell they didn't host if she knows the coats go in the bedroom.

"Sure." I nod to Lee, and he walks down my hallway to the second bedroom. I move to the kitchen, Shayna following me. "Do you guys want something to drink?"

"That'd be great," Shayna says.

I turn to face her as she sets a gift bag I didn't realize she was holding on the counter by the stove.

"What's in there?" I nod at the glittery pink-and-purple bag that looks totally out of place in my industrial kitchen.

"An engagement gift for Brady and Violet."

I swing my gaze Lee's way as he returns from the bedroom. "You didn't tell me I had to get them a gift."

He holds up his hands. "I didn't know. Shayna took care of that."

"You know, if you had a woman in your life, she would help you do these kinds of things," Shayna says in a singsong voice.

I narrow my eyes at her. "Don't start." I swing open the fridge door. "What do you guys want to drink? I've got light and regular."

Shayna peers over my shoulder. "Light or regular what?"

"Beer," I answer, straightening up so she can see around me.

"You don't have any coolers?" Shayna asks.

I look at her. "I have a subzero freezer right here." I point at where it is directly beside the fridge. "Why would I need a cooler?"

She presses her lips together and looks back at Lee, who is already laughing. Fuck them. I didn't want to do this in the first place.

"I think she means wine or vodka coolers," Lee says.

My forehead wrinkles. "Oh… no. Just beer." I motion to

where all the bottles are lined up like soldiers in the large fridge.

"That's okay. I'll just take a light beer then," she says with a tone that suggests she's unhappy.

"Same," Lee echoes.

The doorbell rings and I pass them each a beer. "Here. I'll be back in a second."

Thank God I gave the concierge the names of everyone I'm expecting and directed him to let everyone up; otherwise, I would have to spend half the night answering his calls.

When I swing open the door, Darius and Elijah are arguing about some draft pick. Darius is a defensive end on the team and Elijah is a cornerback, and they both think they know the most about football. They make predictions on trades and always tell the other they don't know what they're talking about.

"You don't know what you're talking about," Elijah says before greeting me with a big smile.

"Hey, guys." I let them in, and we shake hands, then hug, patting each other on the back.

"Hey, hostess with the mostest," Darius says with a laugh.

"No thanks to you two."

When we took a vote in the locker room as to who should host tonight, both these pricks voted for me.

Eli claps his hand on my shoulder. "C'mon, it can't be that bad."

"Yeah? Next time you host something, and we'll exchange notes." I arch an eyebrow.

"All right, whenever you get engaged, I promise I'll host the engagement party." Eli grins, slaps Darius on the back, and the two crack up all the way into my kitchen.

"Har har. We all know me getting engaged is about as likely as Darius here winning a round of poker."

Eli points at Darius, who scowls, and I laugh.

"You guys have jokes, huh?" He's always on the losing end of our poker games.

"Beer is in the fridge, and food is on the counter. Which reminds me, I gotta order the pizza."

The two of them share a look with raised eyebrows.

"What?" I ask.

"Nothing." Darius presses his lips together. "Pizza's good, man."

I cross my arms and look down my nose at them. "Is there something wrong with pizza?"

"I love pizza," Eli says. "But it's also what my sister orders for my niece and nephew's birthday parties. I don't think it's usually something to serve at an engagement party."

"When my sister got engaged, everything was mini. Mini crab cakes, mini wieners wrapped in dough, mini shrimp thing on a cracker." Darius looks at Eli. "I did love those mini wieners though." He stares into space as if remembering them fondly. "Pizza is cool though."

Eli covers his mouth and bends over. "Please stop with the wieners. You're just asking for it."

"You're so immature!" Darius opens the fridge, helping himself to a beer.

Another knock on the door and my arms drop to my sides. "Well, consider me a trendsetter." I brush past them toward the door.

"Hey, man," Miles, the team's safety, says when I open the door. "Fed up already?"

"You have no idea," I grumble, opening the door wider.

Miles glances down the hall. "Great," he mutters and pushes in past me. "I need a drink."

I peek my head out into the hall, although I already know only one person gets Miles all riled up. Sure enough, Bryce is sauntering down the hallway. She works for the San Jose newspaper, and she and Miles go together about as well as ice cream and relish, though no one really knows why.

"Miles hiding out from me?" she says when she reaches me. She, too, holds a gift bag, along with another big bag slung over her shoulder.

"Guess so." She's friends with Shayna and now Violet, which is why I had to invite her.

"Hey!" Shayna says behind me and rushes over to give Bryce a hug, Lee behind her.

"Can I get you a beer?" I ask Bryce.

"There's light beer or regular beer," Shayna says in what sounds to me like a sarcastic tone.

Bryce chuckles and pulls a bottle of wine from the large bag she's carrying. "Please. When I found out who the host was, I knew I had to come prepared." She winks in my direction.

Shayna quickly thrusts her beer into Lee's hands. "You're going to share, right?"

"Of course." Bryce smiles and they venture into the kitchen.

Lee shrugs and finishes her beer.

Halfway to the kitchen, Shayna turns around. "Chase, where do you keep your wineglasses?"

I arch a brow at her.

"Right. No wineglasses. Solo cups it is." She salutes me and continues to the kitchen.

I groan. "This is a fucking nightmare."

"Could be worse," Lee says with a smug smile I want to punch off his fucking face.

"Oh yeah, how?"

"You could be hosting a baby shower."

I scowl. "Fuck off."

Then I walk over to the coffee table where I left my phone, pull up the app, and order the pizza. Once I've ordered, there's another knock at the door. For the next twenty-five minutes, I spend my time answering the door and offering drinks, doing my best not to act as if having all these people in my private space doesn't feel like fire ants crawling up my ass.

I'm standing near my door, shooting the shit with a few of the guys on the team, when I hear people talking out in the hall. It sounds like Brady. What the hell is he doing making a ruckus out there? He's the guest of honor, and I'm pretty sure the sooner he gets in here, the sooner all these people leave.

I excuse myself and walk over to the door, whipping it open. "Thought I heard you out here. What the hell, are you trying to piss off all my—" I abruptly stop talking when I notice Miles's sister, Twyla, standing with Brady and Violet.

What the hell is she doing here?

"Funny thing, we just met your new neighbor." Brady thumbs toward Twyla.

My stomach lurches. Great, as if tonight could get any worse. Temptation just moved in across the hall.

three

. . .

Twyla

Chase fills the doorway of his condo with his mouth hanging open. My brother, Miles, once told me Chase is one of the biggest tight ends in the league and at six foot four, two hundred sixty-five pounds of muscle, I believe him. But that's not what's most intimidating about the man—it's the constant scowl glued on his face whenever he looks at someone and his short, flippant answers on the rare occasion he talks to you.

Still, I'd be lying if I claimed I didn't have a small crush on the man. It wasn't anything I worried about before because I was with Mathew and I was only looking. I may have been taken, but I wasn't dead. Chase truly is the perfect package with his short beard and his trimmed brown hair that's always lighter on the ends. Add on his stacked frame and deep-brown eyes, and he looks drop-dead sexy in his Kingsmen uniform, but he's even sexier dressed in regular clothes, like right now.

And I cannot believe he's my across-the-hall neighbor.

"Hey, Chase." I smile widely at him since my arms are immobile from holding a box.

He recovers from whatever stupor he's in, blinking a few

times and nodding briskly. "Hey… so you live here now?" He motions toward the door directly across the hall from his.

"For the next few months. I'm condo slash pet-sitting for a tech guy who's in Asia for a while."

The four of us stand awkwardly for a beat, then Brady widens his eyes at Chase.

Chase glances at me as if I'm the last kid waiting to be picked in gym class. "You gonna join us?"

I cringe. "Thing is… my brother doesn't know yet that I've moved here. And I doubt a party is the best place to tell him."

"Nonsense. Your brother will be excited to see you. Right, Chase?" Violet says.

He clears his throat. "Yeah, sure."

That isn't exactly a ringing endorsement. But it *would* be nice to see everyone after my long trip.

"Okay, I just have to put this in the condo, and then I'll come over." I motion with the box toward condo number 3311 behind me.

"Chase can take that box for you so you can open the door. Right, buddy?" Brady claps him on the shoulder, walking past him.

"Last I checked, you had two hands," Chase mumbles.

"Guest of honor, my friend." Brady walks into Chase's condo.

Violet follows her fiancé but glances over her shoulder at us.

"Do you mind?" I ask Chase, lifting the box.

"Here." He holds out his hands for the box, and I pass it over.

"Thanks." I fish the key for the condo out of my purse, open the door, and hold it for Chase.

"Nice place." He walks in and sets the box on an expensive-looking table in the entryway. "It's really… modern."

"You've never been in here before? I figured you would have since you're neighbors."

"I'm not really the neighborly kind of guy. I saw this guy twice, maybe."

I glance around the stark, gray-on-gray condo filled with modern furniture that looks as comfortable as plastic blow-up furniture. "Yeah, it's not really my taste, but there are worse places to live for a few months, that's for sure."

Chase stiffens and stares at the corner.

"*Meow*." The owner's Persian cat pops around the corner.

I get down on my haunches. "Hey, Kiwi. Come here, sweetie." I hold my hand out for her to nuzzle, but she goes right over to Chase and weaves through his legs.

Kiwi's got great taste. Can't blame her. Given the two of us, I'd choose him too.

Chase looks pale and unsure of what he should do.

"Are you allergic?"

"No," he bites out.

"Do you just not like animals?" I tilt my head.

"I like animals just fine. Dogs, I get. I grew up with them, see their purpose. What's the point of these hairballs?"

I gasp and pick up Kiwi, who meows in protest as though she is really enjoying rubbing herself against the big football player. *I get it, girl. I wouldn't mind rubbing myself on him too.* "The point is companionship. And cuddles. And every cat is different. They all have their own personalities, just like dogs." I turn my attention to the white puff ball in my arms. "Don't you listen to him, Kiwi. He doesn't know what he's talking about."

"If you say so," Chase grumbles and glances toward the door as if he's afraid someone might have locked him in here.

"Thanks for your help. I guess it's time for me to face the music with Miles." I bend and set down Kiwi.

She trots away with her chin in the air as though we've personally offended her.

Chase holds the door open for me. "Miles likes when you're here. It'll be fine."

"I'm hoping for a better reaction than fine." I pocket the key and leave my purse on the table beside the box. When I walk past Chase, I inhale a whiff of his cologne and fight the urge to lean in to inhale deeper. Whatever he's wearing has a fresh outdoorsy scent that perfectly suits him.

I wait for him to let us into his place, and I'm not two steps into the condo before Miles and I spot one another. He's standing just inside the door with a beer in his hand, talking to a guy who I think is a trainer for the team.

As soon as Miles sees me, he excuses himself from the conversation and walks over to me, arms open. "Twyla? What are you doing here?"

He envelops me in a hug as he always does when we haven't seen each other in a while.

"Surprise," I say, pulling away with a big smile.

"I'm so happy you're here. Did Violet tell you about the party?"

I shake my head. "No, it's kind of a fluke that I'm here. I have something to tell you."

His eyes narrow slightly, probably thinking it has something to do with Mathew.

"I had to get away from Connecticut and from everyone giving me sad puppy-dog eyes every time I saw them. I just needed a change. So, I... moved here!"

He doesn't say anything at first, and I'm unsure if he's processing the information or if he's mad. "What about your teaching job?"

"They granted me a leave of absence, given the circumstances. I guess that's one good thing about your boss being your godfather?" A small chuckle leaves my lips, but not his.

"Oh, well, that's good. I wish you'd told me though. I would've had the house cleaner get the guest room set up for you."

I wave off his concern. "I won't be staying with you. I took a job house-sitting for some tech executive."

He blinks a few times in surprise, then stares for a long stretch. "Seems like you've got it all sorted out."

"I'm sorry I didn't tell you. It was a bit of an impulsive move on my part, and I wasn't sure how you'd feel about it. I promise I won't cramp your style while I'm here."

"Cramp my style? What are you talking about? C'mon, squirt." He tugs me into him, wrapping his arm around me. "You know I love it when you're here."

"Yeah, but a short visit is different than having your little sister around when you're trying to pick up women and hang out with your friends." I pull away and gesture around the room.

Miles glances at someone behind me and back at me. "There's not too much of that going on these days. There's an epidemic of people falling in love around here." He laughs, but I wonder if it bugs him.

"I just heard the news!" I turn and Bryce and Shayna are beelining over to me. "Violet just told us you're here for a while." Bryce pulls me into a hug.

Then Shayna does the same. "This is so exciting!"

Having a welcome like that from friends I've met through my brother feels really good after everything back home.

"We're gonna have so much fun," Bryce says, then glances at Miles. "No matter what big bro here says."

I laugh. One of the draws about moving here was spending more time with Shayna, Bryce, and Violet.

"Big bro says that you'd better not get her into any trouble," Miles says, looking at Bryce as if he's a police officer letting her go with a warning.

Bryce rolls her eyes.

"I couldn't believe it when Violet told us where you're living. What are the chances?" Shayna shakes her head and smiles, then takes a sip from her Solo cup, eyeing all of us over the rim of her glass.

Creases form on Miles's forehead. "What does that mean?"

"She lives across the hall from Chase now. Like, *right* across the hall." Bryce looks delighted, telling my brother this information.

I don't know what the deal is with those two. It's clear neither of them like the other, but they both get off on poking the other.

He looks to me for confirmation, and I nod. "I ran into Brady and Violet in the elevator. That's how I found out about this party."

My brother looks as though he doesn't know how to feel about this development.

"You're probably really happy, right, Miles? I mean… now Chase can keep a *really* good eye on your sister. We all know how overprotective you are of her," Bryce says.

Miles's jaw clenches.

"Okay, you two, retreat into your separate corners," Shayna says, clearly seeing, as I am, that Bryce is trying to upset him.

"Are you sure you're okay with me being here?" I ask Miles, pressing my lips together while I wait for him to answer.

He smiles at me. "Of course I am. It's gonna be great."

He pulls me into another side hug, and though I want to believe him, something about his tone rings different.

four

. . .

Chase

"What do you think, Chase?"

"Huh?" I blink and tear my eyes away from the petite, long-haired brunette who's been stealing my attention all night.

Not that she's been trying to. Twyla's just being her usual self, lighting up the room and flitting from group to group, leaving nothing but sunshine and smiles in her path.

Jesus, if my old man could hear me now, he'd have me committed.

"Do you think we can go all the way this year?" Brady asks me.

"Course we can. If Burrows can manage to not get injured, we'll be good."

Lee shoots me the finger, then takes a pull off his beer. "So… kinda weird that Twyla's your neighbor now, huh?"

"That's one word for it." I bring my own beer to my lips.

Brady barks out a laugh.

"What's that about?" My eyebrows furrow.

"Oh nothing," he says, all innocent, as if there's not a shit-eating grin on his face.

"You got something to say, say it."

Brady straightens. "All right, I will. I think you have the hots for her." He looks around to the others for confirmation that they think the same.

"You're outa your fucking mind." I scowl.

"If you say so."

"He has a point. You've barely taken your eyes off her," Lee says.

"Bullshit."

"Your eyes have practically been glued to her ass all night," Brady adds.

My hand clenches around my beer so tightly I'm afraid the glass might break. "That's Miles's little sister, assholes."

"Did I hear my name?" Miles walks up, all smiles, clearly having no idea what we're discussing. If he did, he'd have my balls in a vise grip from these guys even suggesting what they are—whether they're right or not.

"We were just wondering when you and Bryce are gonna sleep together and get rid of all the sexual tension between you guys." Brady claps him on the shoulder.

What's up with this guy? He gets engaged and decides to call everyone out on why they aren't with someone?

Miles shakes his head with a look of disgust. "That pussy's poison."

"You're saying that like you know firsthand." Lee arches his eyebrow.

Before Miles can respond, Violet pokes her head between Brady and Lee. "Mind if I borrow my fiancé for a few minutes, boys?"

Brady wraps his arms around her shoulders. "What's up?"

"We should probably say a few words… thank everyone for coming." She places a quick kiss on his lips.

His hand slides down, and he pats her ass. "You got it." Brady looks at the three of us. "Excuse me, gentlemen, duty calls."

They move to the far end of the room and stand in front of

the TV mounted on the wall. Brady tries to get everyone to quiet down, and when that doesn't work, Violet has him hold her drink, puts her pinkie fingers in her mouth, and lets loose with the loudest whistle I've ever heard. It rivals the one Coach wears around his neck during practices.

Everyone stops what they're doing and turns their attention to the front of the room.

"Sorry to interrupt everyone's good time, but Brady and I wanted to say a few words," Violet says. "First we want to thank Chase for hosting tonight."

"Yeah, we know you didn't want to do it, but *A* for effort. Next time, maybe consider getting a caterer," Brady adds, and Violet playfully smacks him on the arm while I scowl. "Seriously though, I know opening up your private space to everyone is not at the top of your list of things you want to do, so we really appreciate it."

I shove my free hand into the front pocket of my jeans and nod at him.

"I don't come from a big family, but I always wished I did." Violet looks out over everyone. "And I'm starting to realize what a big family this team is. I want to thank all of you for making me feel comfortable as the newbie of the group. Especially because I didn't know the difference between a touchdown and first down."

Chuckles ring through the crowd.

"I'm so happy this woman agreed to marry me when I asked," Brady says. "And I'm even more happy that all of you get to be a part of this and, of course, our big day." Brady carries on, talking about how much Violet means to him.

I grow bored listening to this bullshit and look around at everyone else to see if they feel the same. But everyone is smiling and seemingly enjoying this long-winded speech as Brady extols the virtues of his bride-to-be. Then my gaze snags on one person in particular.

Twyla stands near the back of the crowd, and though I can

tell she's trying her best to smile at the happy couple, it comes off as more of a grimace. She's fiddling with her hands in front of her, and her full lips are pressed into a thin line.

I frown.

She dips her head and disappears down the hall that leads to the bedrooms.

I don't know what possesses me to follow her, but I do. And when I get to the end of the hallway and find her at the far end with her back to me, trying to wiggle the locked door handle of my second spare bedroom, I react without thinking.

"What the hell are you doing?" I bark, eating up the distance between us in a few strides.

She startles, her shoulders practically going up to her ears, and spins around. "I was looking for the bathroom."

I've never felt like a bigger asshole and that's saying something. I've had more than my fair share of asshole moments in my lifetime, but this is the biggest.

Tears track down her face and she quickly swipes at them with her small hands. Then she tilts her head up as if daring me to comment.

"Bathroom's through here." I motion to the door just behind me to my right.

"Great, thanks." She pushes past me and disappears into the bathroom, shutting the door.

Great. Now what do I do? Pretend I don't know that she's upset and move on with my night or wait here until she emerges so I can see what the problem is?

I am not the man to console an upset woman. I'm an only child with hardly any extended family, and I grew up on a ranch in Montana, spending most of my time alone. I'm not exactly well versed in feelings and interpersonal relationships.

"Fuck," I mutter and push my hand through my hair. I start back down the hall to go listen to Brady drone on some more, but something stops me in my tracks.

Something about letting her come out of that bathroom and finding me long gone, not giving a shit about how upset she is, doesn't sit right, so I spin around and lean against the wall opposite the bathroom door, waiting with my arms crossed.

I probably look more like a bouncer at a nightclub than a confidant, but it's the best I can do. I'm certainly not going to wrap her up in a bear hug and let her cry on my shoulder. It's what a woman like Twyla deserves, but I'm not the guy to give it to her. Not just because her older brother is one of my best friends, but because I'd like having her body that close to me too much. There's no sense in getting dumb ideas about things that can never be reality.

The door opens and Twyla stops in the doorway of the bathroom, her jaw open as she stares at me.

"What's wrong?" I ask.

She shakes her head but stares at the floor. "Nothing. I just had a moment. I'm fine."

"Bullshit. You ran out crying. Just tell me what's wrong."

She sighs and her shoulders sag. "Ever since Mathew called off our engagement… I don't know. Sometimes it's hard to see other couples so happy. It's hard not to think back to my own engagement party and how happy and hopeful I was and now… well, let's say I never thought it'd turn out like this." She brings her hands up to cover her face. "I feel horrible saying that."

"Don't." I pull her hands away from her face. "Own how you feel. Don't apologize for it."

"I'm really happy for Violet and Brady, I am." She sounds as if she's trying to convince me or something.

"Twyla, I don't care whether you are or you're not. That asswipe Mathew"—Jesus, I hate even saying that guy's name—"did you wrong. It's okay to be pissed about it and feel whatever else you're feeling."

The look of concern on her face morphs into a small smile.

Though it's a little sadder than her usual smile, I almost rub my chest from the warm feeling of being the one to put it there.

"Thanks," she says. "For not judging me."

I raise my hands. "Judgment-free zone."

She meets my gaze and I can't for the life of me strip it away. "Good to know."

"There you are," Bryce says from the entrance to the hallway. "I've been looking for you."

I'm starting to understand why Miles finds this woman so irritating. Her timing sucks.

"I was just using the bathroom." Twyla thumbs behind her.

"Shayna, Violet, and I are going to go out next week and you have to come." She loops her arm through Twyla's and drags her down the hallway back toward the party.

Since I'm unable to divert my attention, I catch when Twyla looks back over her shoulder at me. There's that damn feeling in my chest again.

Fucking heartburn.

five

. . .

Twyla

The day after the engagement party, my brother calls to ask if I want to meet up with him. He's totally doing a welfare check on me, but I agree because I love hanging out with Miles.

I love the outdoors, but I'm not a big fan of the cold. Living in Connecticut meant I spent the majority of the year inside. Since it's a beautiful September day, I suggest that we meet at Golden Gate Park. Miles agrees, and after some snuggles with Kiwi, I head out.

I spot my brother a few minutes after I arrive, his baseball cap and sunglasses in place. This is pretty typical if we're going to be lingering in public. It's not like he's the world's biggest movie star, but fans do recognize him, especially during football season.

"Warding off all your adoring fans?" I ask with humor.

He pulls me into a hug. "You know it."

When we separate, we walk down the pathway farther into the park.

"Talked to Mom and Dad this morning," he says.

I nod. "I figured. I asked them not to tell you I was here until I had a chance to see you."

"That's what Mom said. I can't believe you thought I'd be pissed you were coming here to live. What kind of brother do you think I am?" he asks with mock offense.

"The best kind." I bump him with my elbow. "But you have your own life, and I've only ever been a temporary distraction here. Most guys don't want their little sisters cramping their style long term."

He laughs. "I don't have much of a style for you to cramp."

"You're a professional football player. I'm sure you could have as much *style* as you wanted."

He shrugs as we walk around an elderly couple holding hands. "Sure, but you know me. I'm not interested in clout-chasers. When I'm ready to settle down, I need a woman whose mind turns me on as much as her body."

"They can't be that impossible to find." I glance at him.

He doesn't answer right away, looking pensive. "Not impossible, no. But pretty damn difficult."

"Well, I'm sure it'll happen when you least expect it."

"Yeah, maybe. What about you? You think you'll start dating again soon?" He leads us toward the Shakespeare Garden.

"No, Miles, I'm not going to start dating soon."

"Why not? You've already given enough of your life to that piece of shit. You need to start getting on with life without him."

I attempt to stem my anger as we pass through the iron gates and the archway into the garden. "I understand what you mean, but just because Mathew proved himself to be a douchebag doesn't mean I'm not still mourning the loss of the future I thought I'd have with him. It takes time, and I'm not ready to move on with someone else."

We sit on a bench and watch a small group of older adults do tai chi.

"I get it, I get it." My brother squeezes my shoulder. "I just want to see you happy again."

I sigh. "I know. I'm getting there, I am. It just takes time. Being here will help give me some distance from everything that went down."

He nods and looks off into the distance. "I know I can be overbearing at times—"

"You?" I bring my hand to my chest in dramatic fashion. "I hadn't noticed."

"Brat." He nudges me with his elbow. "I worry about you is all. It took everything I had not to hop on a plane and beat the shit out of that bastard."

I lay my head on his shoulder. "I know you do. You've always thought it was your job to look out for me."

There was a time in my life when I needed that, and I appreciated it then. It's not that I don't appreciate it now, but sometimes Miles has trouble remembering I'm a grown adult who can make her own decisions.

"It's my job. But I'll try to back off a bit. Especially now that you're not marrying that piece of shit."

I pop up off his shoulder and narrow my eyes at him. "You don't have to sound so happy about it."

"Better to find out what he's really like before you're married rather than ten years and two kids in."

I sigh. "True enough."

"Listen, why don't you come to our practice tomorrow? Shayna will be there, and sometimes Violet brings Theo."

"And what about Bryce?" I know she covers a lot of the practices for the paper.

His jaw tics. "Yeah, she'll probably be there too."

"What's the deal with you two anyway?" I shift to face him and study his reaction.

"There is no deal." He stands from the bench. "She's a pain in the ass and only out for number one—herself. C'mon, let's go check out the Japanese Garden."

I drop the subject because I don't want to ruin our day. He obviously doesn't want to talk about her. Besides, I just told him he should stop digging around in my life, so I shouldn't dig around in his.

———

I return from the park and enter the lobby as Chase steps off the elevator.

Because it would be weird to pass him without saying anything, I stop when he's within a few feet of me and smile. "Hey, Chase."

He glances up from the phone in his hand and backtracks a step, his head shaking slightly. I guess he didn't see me. "Hey, Twyla." He shoves his phone into his back pocket.

"Thanks for letting me crash your party last night."

"Yeah, no problem." He shifts in place and glances toward the door.

"Sorry about the waterworks." My cheeks heat with embarrassment, but somehow it feels like it would be weirder if I didn't mention the fact that he caught me crying last night. Now that I think of it, it was actually sort of sweet that he hung around outside the bathroom to make sure I was okay.

"It's not a big deal. Don't mention it." He says that last sentence as though if I mention it again, he'll cause me harm. As if the mere mention of me having feelings of any kind makes him uncomfortable.

We stand there for a moment, not saying a word, and things become awkward fast.

It's then that I realize this is the first time the two of us have ever been alone together. Though it's no secret that Chase isn't a big conversationalist, I'm realizing just how much he doesn't bother with mundane chitchat.

"Where are you headed?" I ask cheerily, searching for anything to beat back the weird tension between us.

Apparently, that was not the question to ask to start a conversation because he grimaces and rubs his short facial hair with his palm. "Out."

"Sorry, I wasn't prying." Maybe he's off to hook up with someone or something. From what Miles says, Chase is really private about his personal life.

The idea of him going off to meet some other woman makes my stomach sour, but it's none of my business.

"Nah, I'm sor—"

I raise my hand. "You don't have to explain. I should go up anyway. Kiwi's probably looking for her dinner."

When I go to move past him, to my surprise, he grabs my wrist. His hand is so large it's like a bear paw. I stare down at it, and he runs his thumb over the inside of my wrist. I look up at him, but he doesn't say anything. He looks as though he wants to, but maybe he doesn't know what to say?

"Miles invited me to practice tomorrow, so maybe I'll see you there."

After he continues not to say anything, I smile, giving him an easy out for our awkward encounter. He nods and drops my wrist.

I beeline to the elevator and stab at the button. I'm not sure what that was between us, but one thing is clear—I don't want to know either.

six

. . .

Chase

Lee and I toss the football back and forth while Coach Baker talks to the coaching staff before our drills and scrimmage.

I spotted Twyla in the stands as soon as I came out onto the field. Of course I did, because she's like a goddamn beacon to me. I force myself not to look in her direction. I was a complete asswipe after our run-in yesterday in the lobby, but I was caught off guard, and when she asked where I was headed, I clammed up. It's going to take me time to realize she's staying across the hall from me, and we'll have run-ins in the common areas.

My hands are up to catch Lee's pass when Miles runs in front of me, intercepting the ball.

"What the hell was that?" I put my hands on my hips.

"I need to talk to you." He tosses the ball back to Lee and holds his finger up in a one-minute gesture to him.

Oh great, what could this be about?

My eyebrows draw together. "What's up?" Please tell me Twyla isn't complaining to her big brother about how rude I was to her yesterday.

"I wanted to ask you to do me a favor." He glances over my shoulder at Twyla sitting in the stands.

When I look back too, she looks uncomfortable. Her eyes bobble around, then concentrate on her phone.

"Depends." I cross my arms.

"I'm wondering if you could take Twyla to the gala as your plus-one." He smiles wide, showing off those prince-like pearly whites that make the fans put him in the boy-next-door category.

I just about choke on my tongue. Is Miles seriously asking me to take his sister on a *date*?

The Kingsmen hold a big fancy charity gala every year, and though I don't hate doing charitable work, I do hate getting dressed in a penguin suit and parading around, talking to a bunch of people I don't care for and taking pictures for the press.

I scowl. "You can't take her?"

Miles shakes his head. "I already asked someone, otherwise I would."

"What? You have some secret girlfriend no one knows about?" I arch an eyebrow.

He shakes his head again. "Just this girl I've gone on a few dates with. It's not serious, but I don't want to screw it up by uninviting her in case it could lead somewhere. I asked her before Twyla moved to town."

"How do you know I don't have a date?" I give him my best stare-down. They all assume, but I could be dating someone.

He laughs. "You never have a date. In fact, in all the years we've played together, I've never seen you date anyone."

He has a point. I mostly do hookups and never with football fans because who needs the goddamn headache? And I've never brought a girl I'm hooking up with around the guys. It would give her the wrong impression—that what we were doing meant something.

"Why is it so important to you that she goes?"

He sighs, and concern washes over his features. "I don't want her sitting at home by herself while everyone she knows in town is out having fun. She follows all of us on social media and she'll see us in all the tagged photos. She's had a crappy couple of months and I'm trying to help her get out of the funk."

I run my hand over the back of my neck and look at the ground. The idea of Twyla sitting in that condo, upset and pining after her ex, makes me want to deflate a football with my hands. Still, I'm not convinced I'm the one to show her a good time.

But the image of Twyla crying at Brady's engagement party resurfaces, and I already know my answer.

"Fine. I'll do it. It's not a real date though."

Miles laughs. "Yeah, no shit. That's why I'm asking you. Anyone else on the team and I'd have to worry that they'd try to sleep with her."

The idea of Twyla and me in bed together is enough to keep me from responding to his comment. "Can we please get back to work now?"

He claps me on the shoulder. "Thanks again. Oh, and will you do me another favor?"

"You're pushing it."

"Keep an eye on her? Let me know if there're any guys skulking around that I should know about."

The corners of my mouth pinch together, and I nod. Just what I want to do—playdate and babysitter to the woman I'm doing my best to avoid, for both our sakes.

———

After we finish our drills, Coach tells us to head to lunch. I walk to the sidelines to grab a drink before going into the training facility to eat, and as I'm squirting water into my mouth, Miles steps up beside me.

"What now?" I set down the water bottle.

"I'm gonna go talk to Twyla about the gala, c'mon." He nods in the direction she was sitting, which is empty. She's now walking down the stands.

My gaze flicks back to meet his. "You mean she doesn't know you hooked her up with a date? I assumed you'd already OK'd it with her."

He waves off my concern. "It'll be fine. She likes you." Then he walks toward her.

I grumble and follow him. Great. What if Twyla doesn't want to go with me? What if she'd rather go with any guy on the team other than me? I'm not an idiot, I know I'm not exactly Mr. Personality. But I don't get any time to voice my concerns to Miles because before I know it, we're standing in front of her.

Twyla's wearing a pair of tight jeans and a casual white button-up shirt with white sneakers. Her hair is more wavy than curly today and she smiles at us as though she hasn't a care in the world.

"Hey, guys. You must be beat. That's a workout." She wipes the sweat from her forehead.

"We still have a scrimmage this afternoon. You're going to stick around, eat with us, and watch, right?"

She hems and haws. "I should probably get going. I have to feed Kiwi." When Miles's eyebrows draw down, she adds, "The cat I'm watching."

"Right. Okay, well, listen, I talked to Chase, and he's going to take you to the gala. Sorry, I have a date this year."

Way to just throw it out there, Miles.

Her mouth drops open and her eyes widen, and she quickly turns to me. The expression reminds me of the deer's eyes when I hit it on the highway back in high school.

"Try to contain your excitement," I say.

"You had a good time whenever I've brought you and everyone's going to be there."

Miles doesn't spell out the fact that he doesn't want her sitting at home alone, but she's not an idiot. She knows exactly why he's setting up dates for her.

"You're usually the one trying to sabotage my dates, not make them for me," she says.

"Because this isn't a real date; it's with Chase." He bops her on the end of her nose with his finger as though she's a toddler, and she rolls her eyes.

I don't know how she doesn't get tired of his shit.

"So this woman you asked, is it serious?" she asks Miles.

"You sound like Mom. I'm gonna go eat. Give me a call later, all right?" He tugs her into his side and kisses the top of her head.

I can't help but wonder what her hair smells like. In my experience, women have two kinds of scents: floral or berry. I wonder which one she is.

"Will do." She smiles and watches him go, but as soon as he's out of earshot, she faces me again, head angled to the side. "Chase, you don't have to take me to the gala. It's really nice that you agreed to as my brother's friend, but I'm not going to impose on your night out. You should go with someone you're into."

I swallow hard. I can't tell her I *would* be going with someone I'm into. That's something she'll never know. Something Miles will never know.

"Don't worry about it." My voice comes out gruffer than I intend.

"No, really. I'll be fine." She rests her hand on my forearm.

God, she's so tiny compared to me.

"I wasn't asking anyone else anyway."

She blinks rapidly a couple of times and her head swivels back. "Oh… okay. Still though, I don't want a pity invite." The corners of her lips tip down, and I realize how much I hate seeing her upset. She's almost always smiling and happy.

I step forward, moving closer to her so that she has to rear her head back to look up at me. "No pity involved. Any guy should be honored to have you on their arm for a night."

She swallows hard as she maintains my gaze. "As long as you're sure you don't mind."

"I don't mind, Twyla." I turn to leave, take a few steps, then turn around. "In case I don't see you before then—I'll knock on your door at five thirty the night of the gala."

She smiles and nods. I walk away, already knowing I'm knee-deep in shit.

seven

. . .

Twyla

For the next week, I don't run into Chase once. Not by the mailboxes, not entering or exiting the building, nor in the elevator. I'm not sure if that's by his design or just a coincidence, but I'm oddly disappointed every time I step into the hallway or the lobby and he's not there.

So, by 5:25 the evening of the gala, my nerves are shot. Chase said he didn't mind taking me, but it's hard not to feel like a pitiful little girl whose brother set her up—especially since it's not even a real date. The idea of someone spending time with me because they feel obligated, not because they want to… well, let's just say I've spent a lot of time wondering how long my ex-fiancé wanted to bail on our engagement before he finally said something.

But I decide not to focus on the negativity Mathew left me with and instead have a good time tonight. Moping around won't change the fact Chase is taking me because Miles asked him.

I went shopping with Shayna this week and found a dress, a pale-blue chiffon A-line dress with a halter and high neck and a slit up the front of the dress. Half my hair is piled up in curls on top of my head, and the rest hangs down my back.

I'm wearing more makeup than I normally do. Overall, I have a classy, polished look.

I don't know what Chase's type is, but I'm sure I'm not it. Being the little sister of his teammate takes me out of the running immediately.

Not that I should be thinking about what his type is anyway. I'm still grieving my future with Mathew, although truthfully, I hate him more and more every day.

The doorbell rings and I smooth the front of my dress, drawing in a deep breath. The walk to the door is excruciatingly long, and when I swing open the door, I can't put into words the feelings rushing through my body. It's not that I haven't seen Chase's six foot four-inch frame in a tuxedo—I've been to the gala before—but it will take anyone's breath away every time.

"Hey," I say, opening the door a little wider so he can step in.

His eyes roam up and down my body and when he sees me notice, he looks apologetic. "Hey." We stand there awkwardly for a beat, and when I think he might compliment how I look, he says, "You ready to go?"

Disappointment tumbles through my stomach like a bowling ball plopping down the stairs, but I keep my smile in place. "Just let me grab my purse and coat."

He takes the door from me, and I hurry over to the front closet where my coat is hanging, slip it on, and grab my purse off the entry table. "All set."

Chase doesn't say anything, holding the door open for me. We walk in silence down the long hallway toward the elevator.

God, will it be this awkward all night? I open my mouth to speak, but he beats me to it.

"I got us a car for the night so neither one of us would have to worry about driving. It's waiting downstairs."

We stop in front of the elevator, and he hits the down button.

"That was thoughtful of you. Thanks."

He gives me what almost counts as a tight-lipped smile, then looks forward, waiting for the elevator. I think we both breathe a sigh of relief when the elevator dings and the doors slide open.

That lasts for about three seconds until we find ourselves standing in the confined space alone together with nothing to say.

I don't know why it's like this. I've been around him plenty of times and never felt nervous. I know it's me who's putting this energy out there and it needs to stop. Things don't have to be weird between us just because I have a silly crush on him and I'm single now. Chase is always a gentleman with me—albeit a grumpy gentleman. I have to stop reading into signs that aren't there.

With that in mind, I turn to face him. "Do you usually bid on anything in the silent auction?"

He sort of grunts and continues looking straight ahead. "There's not usually anything I'd want to bid on."

I nod, trying to come up with another topic. "Kiwi shit on her owner's bed today."

His head whips in my direction, his warm eyes wide. Finally, a reaction.

"She must miss him and is showing her anger. Thank God I'm sleeping in the guest room."

He chuckles, and though I can tell he's holding back and it's not a full smile, warmth spreads in my chest. "One of our cows got in the house once and left a mud pie in the middle of the living room. My mom was livid."

I cover my mouth and gasp. "How did the cow get in your house?"

He shakes his head and looks as if he's reliving a good

memory. "My cousin left the back door open by accident and one of the cows got past the fence."

"Maybe I should be thankful I only have to clean up the mess with one hand and not a shovel."

He lifts his eyes to meet mine and I suck in a breath when his lips spread in a smile. We're snug in our bubble until the elevator door dings and he motions for me to get out first.

I do and am acutely aware of the way my hips sway as I walk ahead of him. In all the years Mathew and I were together, I never once thought about how I moved as I walked in front of him.

My heels click across the lobby, and he catches up with me in two long strides. The doorman opens the door for us as we approach. A blacked-out SUV waits at the curb, and Chase steps ahead and opens the door for me. I nod a thank-you and duck inside. Once Chase is in the back and the door is closed, the driver eases away from the curb.

"Thanks again for taking me as your plus-one."

"Stop thanking me. I told you it's fine," Chase says in a gruff voice.

"Well, I'm saying it anyway. I always have a good time at this event and it wouldn't have been the end of the world if I didn't go, but I'm happy I don't have to miss it. It'll be fun."

"If you say so." He glances out the window.

"You don't like events like the gala?" I ask.

He turns his head to look at me. "What's to like about being uncomfortable in a tux all night and talking with a bunch of people you'd rather not talk to about topics you don't give a shit about while a camera is at your side, poised to take your smiling picture?"

A small laugh leaves my lips. "Come on now, you know that's a lie. I don't think I've ever seen you smile in a picture." I jab him with my elbow.

He stares at me, appearing bewildered but almost as if he wants to laugh. "Looking at lots of pictures of me?"

My face flushes hot, but I keep my head raised. "Only the ones with my brother in them." I shrug.

He hmms in assent and turns to look back out the window.

The drive over to the Palace Hotel doesn't take long, so a few minutes later, I'm sliding across the seat to climb out of the SUV. Chase is the first one out when the driver opens the door and he offers me his hand. I accept it, his palm dwarfing mine, and take one step out onto the running board. When I go to take my next step, my heel gets hooked in my dress, and I fall forward with an *oomph*.

Large hands wrap around my rib cage and cradle my fall, gently easing me up until I'm standing on my own.

I glance up and say a breathless "Thanks."

Chase looks down at me, and our eyes meet. His hands are still wrapped around my rib cage, his thumb an inch from the bottom of my breast.

In the months since my breakup with Mathew, I haven't had any physical reaction to any man, so this sensation is somewhat foreign. For many years, the only man who spun butterflies in my stomach was Mathew.

The sound of the SUV pulling away behind me draws us from our frozen state and we back away from each other at the same time. Before either one of us can say anything, my brother steps out of his rental pulled up to the curb.

"Hey guys." Miles flashes us a smile then turns to help his date out of the back seat.

From what Miles tells me, their relationship is nothing serious, but he hasn't thrown in the towel either.

She emerges from the back seat, long, straight blonde hair flowing, curves in all the right places, wearing a black body-con dress that shows off all her assets. She looks amazing. I glance at Chase to see his reaction, but he continues to look bored. Here I was about to be jealous he'd rather have Miles's date on his arm. Damn Mathew for making me second-guess the knockout I am too.

"Heather, this is my little sister, Twyla." Miles motions between us. "Twyla, this is Heather." Heather looks at Chase, and Miles nods. "And the grump is Chase."

I take her hand while Chase grunts and tips his chin up at her as though she's a guy.

"Good to meet you," I say.

"Same." She smiles and looks me over, but something about it feels almost competitive, as though she's sizing me up. Did she not hear the sister part?

I smile wider. "Are you looking forward to tonight?"

She gives a little shrug. "We'll see." Then she turns her back to me and all her attention is on my brother. "Can we get inside? I'm chilly."

He smiles and wraps his arm around her shoulders. "Of course."

I want to tell her that if she wore a coat, she wouldn't be so cold, but I'm sure she didn't wear one so that she could show off her dress.

Chase starts toward the hotel entrance without saying a word, so I hurry to catch up to him. When we get inside, the four of us head to the coat check so I can check my coat, then we make our way to the ballroom entrance.

I'm always in awe of this venue. It was built in the late 1800s—I looked it up after the first time I was here—and has so much Gilded Age luxury and historic architecture I can't imagine anyone could tear their eyes away from the art.

Outside the doors to the ballroom is an area where the football players are expected to get their pictures taken by the press. Chase makes his way in front of the backdrop for the photographers and I hang back, letting him do his thing. When he notices that I didn't follow him over, he turns, a deep groove between his eyebrows, and holds his hand out for me. I swear this man and his caveman communication.

My stomach does a swoop like a dive-bombing plane, and I step forward. "Are you sure?" I whisper. "These will get online, and people will think we're a thing."

He leans down and softly says into my ear, "Are you kidding me? You're the only thing making this remotely bearable." Then he loops his arm through mine.

We probably look like a prom couple more than anything since I'm not leaning into him or placing my hand on his chest, but the heat from our point of contact on my arm seeps into my veins and warms my entire body.

"Can you smile for us, Chase?" one of the photographers calls.

"Take the damn picture," Chase responds and my smile widens.

Miles and Heather are next, so we wait for them. Heather isn't afraid to put her hands all over Miles, smiling wide for the camera. Before I actually vomit, they finish and we all file into the ballroom. Chase keeps his arm looped with mine while we make our entrance, and a small girly part of me wonders if it means anything.

Damn, this isn't the seventh grade. Your brother asked him to take you. Remember that.

I unhook our arms when I spot Brady and Violet approaching.

eight

. . .

Chase

Twyla unhooks her arm from mine as soon as we enter the ballroom. Of course she does. *Because you're making her uncomfortable, you idiot.*

When she didn't want to be in the picture, almost as if she felt as though she wasn't worthy, I wanted to make it clear she was. From what Miles said, that ex of hers really did a number on her, and a woman like Twyla should never feel less than. But I should have dropped her arm right after that. I was being greedy because having her near felt so good.

I'd felt like a dick after walking away from her outside the hotel, but watching Miles's date be dismissive of Twyla when she was trying to be nice made me grind my molars. I was going to say something if I didn't get off that sidewalk, then I'd have Miles to deal with.

I've been unsure all night of what to do with my actions since this isn't a *real* date. But I need to keep my hands to myself, that much is clear. She's Miles's little sister and just coming off a broken engagement.

Violet and Brady approach the four of us as soon as we're through the door, and we all say our hellos. Miles introduces his date. I'm not quite sure what he sees in her. She's way too forthcoming with the men and cold to the women.

Shortly after, Lee and Shayna join us and all the women compliment each other on their dresses.

"Guys, why don't we go get all these lovely ladies their drinks?" Brady says.

I ask Twyla what she wants, and she asks for a glass of moscato. The rest of the guys get their marching orders, and we head over to the bar.

Once we're waiting for the bartender to fulfill our orders, Brady turns to his right, looking at Miles and me. "So, is there some new love connection I'm not aware of?"

I roll my eyes but remain tight lipped. I'd figured Miles hadn't mentioned me taking Twyla to anyone because none of the guys had brought it up, but I won't be the one to say anything.

"As if," Miles says. "I'd break his fingers if he ever laid a hand on her."

"You could try," I say, hands flexing into fists at my sides.

"So, what gives?" Brady asks.

Miles shrugs. "I didn't want Twyla sitting at home alone while everyone was at the gala. She's still in a fragile state. Chase never brings anyone to these things, so I asked if Twyla could be his plus-one." He stares down Brady. "You thought that it was a real date? Hell no."

My lips press into a thin line. I know I'm not good enough for his sister, but it's still not fun to hear it out loud in front of my buddies. I play it off though and nod in Miles's direction. "What he said."

"This way, Twyla can hang out with all the other women tonight and have fun and remember that she doesn't need that worthless piece of shit in her life anymore," Miles says.

"Seems like a recipe for disaster," Brady replies.

I narrow my eyes at him.

"What do you mean?" Miles asks with a frown.

"Nothing, forget it." Brady waves it off.

Before anyone can say anything else, the bartender pushes our drinks toward us, and we head back to join the women.

I hand Twyla her glass of wine and she looks at me with a smile that could melt a glacier as she says, "Thanks," with more enthusiasm than a simple drink delivery requires. But that's her, always dazzled by the simplest things.

Bryce makes an excuse to take off almost immediately, saying something about work, leaving Twyla and me with three touchy-feely couples.

Jesus, is this how it's gonna be all the time from now on? Me being the seventh wheel as these guys try to keep their hands off their women?

Twyla must share my sentiment because she turns to me and says, "Want to go check out the silent auction?" The hopeful glint in her eyes tells me she's had enough of playing voyeur too.

"Definitely."

We say our goodbyes, but no one pays us much attention. They'll be asking one another in five minutes where we ventured off to.

"Sorry if you wanted to stay and talk to the guys. I just couldn't handle all the PDA anymore." She looks over her shoulder at me as we worm our way through the tables.

"You're saying that like you think I'm disappointed or something."

"I know you're not really into the auction. It's just the only good excuse I could think of to get out of there."

Once we're through the tables, and without thinking better of it, I place my hand on the small of her back to direct her toward the auction tables. She stiffens when I touch her, so I drop my hand instantly.

I clear my throat. "I was happy to leave them behind. Believe me."

Why can't I remember to keep my hands to myself where

she's concerned? I give myself a mental smack as we approach the tables.

"You planning to bid on anything?" I ask Twyla as we walk down the row, looking over everything.

She looks up at me with a smile. "Not likely. I have a wedding to pay for." When my forehead wrinkles, she explains. "We lost a lot of the deposit money when the wedding was called off, and I plan to pay my parents back for everything they're out of pocket."

What the hell?

While she keeps her smile in place, there's a note of sadness in her voice, even if she does her best to cover it.

"The prick who screwed you over should be the one to pay your parents back."

She shakes her head. "I don't want anything from him. Anyway, I'm determined to pay them back, so I have to pinch pennies." She gestures to her dress. "I found this thing on the clearance rack."

My gaze drifts down and back up her body as my cock twitches. "Good find."

Our eyes lock for a second, then I read the auction card in front of us as though I'm suddenly very interested in an overnight pass at one of the Bay Area's most prestigious spas.

We make our way down the row, commenting here and there about the donations until the emcee comes on the mic to tell everyone to find their seats for dinner. Since we haven't even looked at the seating chart yet, Twyla tasks me with searching the room for her brother and Lee and Brady, whom we're sharing a table with, insisting that my six-four stature gives me the advantage.

She's not wrong. It only takes me a minute to find them at a table on the edge of the dance floor.

I'm not a heathen, so when we reach the table, I pull out Twyla's chair for her and she gives me a bright smile before sitting next to her brother. I end up with Brady on my other side. Brady who keeps acting as if he sees something between Twyla and me.

Dinner barely arrives before the girls are making suggestions to Twyla about what she should do now in her life.

"You need to get back out there. Sow some oats," Bryce says.

"Yeah, just be young and have some fun for a while," Shayna echoes.

My knuckles go white from fisting my silverware, but I don't look up from my plate, worried someone will see my reaction.

"What Twyla needs is to get over that loser she was engaged to and be single for a while," Miles says. "The right guy will come along. There's no rush."

"What do *you* want, Twyla?" Bryce asks. She's obviously not a fan of Miles's overbearing nature with his little sister.

"Honestly, I don't think I'm ready for either probably. I've never…"—she glances beside her at her brother—"been with a guy without being in a relationship, so I'm not sure I could do it and not develop feelings."

Shayna laughs. "Yeah, I wasn't good at it either." She gives Lee a knowing look.

"Thank fuck," he says and leans over to kiss her.

"Same here," Violet says and joins in Shayna's laughter.

"Perfect. Then it's decided. Twyla will stay single for a while," Miles says with a smug look.

Bryce's eyes narrow.

Here we go. Sit back and enjoy the show.

"Who are you to tell her what she can and can't do?" Bryce says to Miles.

He sets his cutlery on either side of his plate as though he's getting ready to fight. "She's my little sister. I want what's best for her."

"We all do," Shayna says as though she took offense.

"But I've known her my whole life. Better than any of you, so I know what's best for her."

"Maybe you're too close to the situation," Bryce says. "You know, forest for the trees and all that."

"They do say the best way to get over someone is to get under someone else," Heather pipes up.

Miles casts an annoyed glance to his right. "Yeah, but—"

"Why don't you guys stop talking like Twyla's not sitting right here and just let her live her damn life however she wants to?" The words fly out of my mouth before I can think better of them.

Everyone at the table is silent for a beat, but I keep cutting my steak, bringing a forkful to my mouth. I feel Twyla's stare on the side of my face, but I don't look at her, afraid to see if she's angry at me for butting in.

The subject quickly changes to our game against Seattle this weekend, and when I finally do have the courage to glance at Twyla, she's not glaring at me like I thought she might. No, she's looking at me in a way that makes it difficult to remember that she's my teammate's little sister and one-hundred-percent off-limits.

nine

. . .

Twyla

Chase Andrews stuck up for me.

The grumpiest man I've ever met put all the strong personalities around this table in their place—for me. I barely remain in my seat instead of wrapping my body around his, kissing his face with thanks.

I'm giddy that a big, burly man told everyone to leave me alone. I shouldn't read too much into it. He was probably just annoyed at listening to everyone go on and on about my love life. I have the impression that Chase prefers a quiet room alone with his thoughts over a roomful of people talking nonstop.

The rest of dinner continues without any more conversation about my love life—something I'm thankful for. I sometimes feel as if that's all anyone ever wants to talk about these days.

Once all the presentations finish and Brady's parents, the owners of the team, have thanked everyone for coming, the music starts. Men around the room stand and hold their hands out to their dates, asking for a dance.

"I'm off to make the rounds," Bryce says and slides out of her chair, dropping her napkin on the seat.

My brother mumbles something and I inwardly roll my eyes that he can't let his issue with Bryce go. What is his problem with her? I've asked before and he never gives a straight explanation.

The rest of us chat for a while, though it's a struggle now that the music is playing until a slow song comes on.

"I love this song," Shayna says to Lee.

Without her having to say anything else, he pushes back his chair and holds out his hand to her before leading her to the dance floor.

"Do you want to dance?" Miles asks Heather, and she happily obliges. That's two gone.

Brady and Violet get pulled away by his parents, who want to introduce them to some people. That leaves Chase and me, side by side, staring at the couples on the dance floor. It only takes about five seconds for the space around us to grow awkward.

Maybe I should excuse myself to use the bathroom, but then he'll picture me peeing. Or I could suggest we get a drink from the bar, but my wineglass is still full. I could say I need to make a phone call but to whom?

Before any of those excuses come out of my mouth, he leans in close to my ear, his breath tickling the bare flesh under my earlobe. "Do you want to dance?"

My stomach goes crazy as though a little gymnast is tumbling inside. "Sure."

He slides out of his chair and comes along to mine, pulling my chair out for me. He doesn't take my hand but motions for me to lead us to the dance floor. I find us a spot on the other side of the dance floor from my brother.

Chase stands there for a moment like a wall barricading a medieval town—tall, intimidating, and immovable. Then he steps into me, and I breathe in his earthy and woodsy cologne. Is this really happening?

He takes me into his arms with care, as if he's trying extra hard to be gentle so he doesn't hurt me, and it sends a rush of emotions through me I can't quite piece together. But when his bear paw of a hand engulfs mine and I wrap one arm around him to lay my hand on his back and feel his hard muscles shift, the feeling fits together—safety.

I am safe in this man's arms.

It wasn't that Mathew didn't make me feel safe or anything, but compared to Chase, I never knew what I was missing with Mathew. Because the feeling right here cannot be overstated. At least not for me. And the fact that it's coming from a huge football player who acts as if he just barely tolerates everyone else's existence in this world makes me feel all the more special.

"Thank you for sticking up for me back there." I crane my head back to look up at him.

He doesn't meet my eyes or even glance down at me. "Everyone needs to worry more about themselves and less about what you want to do with your life. You're a smart girl. You'll figure it out."

If someone snapped a picture of us this instant, I know my cheesy smile would give me away. "You're right."

We dance for another minute, neither speaking a word. I'm trying to keep a respectable distance from him, but every part of me wants to smash myself against him and see what it feels like to have his big, hard body pressed against mine.

"You let your brother push you around too much." His deep voice reverberates in his chest as he circles us around, still not making eye contact.

"It's sort of the dynamic we're used to. Growing up... he looked out for me when things were tough." I stare at his jawline, so sculpted and strong.

His eyes fall to mine for a fleeting moment. "Maybe so. But you're all woman now. You don't need him dictating every aspect of your life for you."

His phrasing skips on a loop in my brain... you're all woman... all woman.

No. Stop. It doesn't mean anything, and even if it did, so what? I just finished telling everyone how I'm not ready for any type of relationship.

"Old habits die hard, I guess."

"Maybe, but you deserve better than that."

A warmness invades my chest again and I look up at him and smile. "You know, you're not as grumpy as you make everyone believe." I slide my hand over his heart. "I think inside here, there's a real softy."

His big hand twitches around mine. "It's just you, Twyla. You bring it out of me."

The slow song ends, and a fast song takes its place. Everyone on the dance floor pulls apart and dances to the fast song, but Chase steps back, removing his hands from me.

"I don't do fast songs." He turns without waiting for me to respond and beelines it off the dance floor.

As I watch him go, I can't help but hope his running has more to do with his words than the song.

———

Chase gives me a wide berth the rest of the night, which is fine. I have a lot of fun with the girls—minus my brother's date. I tried to make small talk with her, like, ten times, to find some common ground, but she didn't seem interested.

I wonder if this is how my brother felt when I started dating Mathew? The difference is that I won't say anything. It's his life and Heather must make him happy somehow, even if I don't see it.

When the event wraps up, Chase and I say our goodbyes and step outside where our ride is waiting for us. Chase waves off the driver and helps me in himself, then we're on our short drive back to the condo building.

"Did you have a good time tonight? I know it's not really your thing…" I ask.

"Better than most." He gives me a tight-lipped smile, which is about the most one can get from him, so I take it as a win.

"What did you think of Heather?"

He looks at me through the corner of his eyes before turning his head directly toward me. "Honestly?"

I nod.

"I don't like her."

I laugh, not at his opinion but at his bluntness. While I worry too much about what other people think, he's firm in his convictions. "Tell me how you really feel."

He shrugs one big shoulder. "You asked."

"I did. The reason I asked is because"—I lean in close—"I feel the same way."

"You don't have to whisper. No one's here." Chase leans into me, one corner of his mouth tugging up.

We're so close, our faces only inches apart, and briefly, I think about pressing my lips to his. Instead, I roll my eyes playfully. "I don't like saying mean things about other people."

He sits back up and I miss his nearness right away. "Why? She certainly wasn't nice to you."

I look down at my hands. I'd noticed the same, obviously, but it wasn't just me. She seemed to think all the women there tonight were her competition, even the engaged ones. Even me, Miles's sister, for crying out loud.

"I don't know, that's just me, I guess."

"Yeah, I know." The way he says it makes it sound as though it's not a good thing. He goes back to looking out the window.

We're quiet for the remainder of the drive, and Chase once again helps me from the back of the SUV once we're parked at the curb. I'm irked when my hand lands in his and my heartbeat picks up.

"Thanks for a fun night," I say as we walk away from the curb, but I stop when I hear something.

"I keep telling—"

I raise my hand for Chase to be quiet and he does, but not without a scowl. I hear the sound again and rush over to the post office box a little farther down the sidewalk.

"What are you doing?" Chase follows me.

I look over my shoulder at him. "Didn't you hear that?"

The little yip sounds again and I think it's coming from under the post office box. I crouch, bending at the waist as I tip my head, supporting myself with my hands. A little orange kitten with big eyes is crouched below the box, meowing and looking scared.

"Twyla, what the hell?"

I ignore Chase. I have to get this little guy or girl out of there.

"C'mere, cutie pie." I reach one hand out close to the base of the mailbox.

At first the kitten steps back, but after ten or twenty seconds, it grows curious enough to walk forward.

"That's it, sweetie. Come closer," I use my most lilting voice. Eventually the kitten is close enough to sniff my hand. When it's done, I pull my hand a little farther back, hoping to coax it out, and reach straight up with my other arm, purse in hand. "Chase, can you hold this for me?"

He takes the purse from my hand, and I get back to work. After about five minutes of coaxing, my legs are on fire, but the kitten is far enough out from under the mailbox that I can scoop it up.

"Are you sure you should be picking up strays?"

I pretend to cover the kitten's ears. "Don't listen to him. He's just a grump."

Then I look at Chase and laugh. The sight of a big guy like

Chase with my evening bag in his hand is actually pretty humorous.

"What?" he grumbles.

"Nice purse." I wink at him, and he rolls his eyes.

"What are you gonna do with that thing?" he asks, eyeing the kitten warily.

"I can't leave it here. I'll have to bring it in for the night. But there's just one thing…"

He frowns. "Nope."

"Chase, I can't bring it to my place." My voice holds a slight whine, but I don't care. Chase is my only hope.

His frown deepens. "Why? He's already got a cat."

"Because it's not my place and also because Kiwi will not take kindly to a new cat in her domain. She might rip it apart."

He frowns and looks down at the little furball meowing in my hands.

"Plus, I doubt this little thing has had any shots. Until it's looked at by a vet, it probably shouldn't be around other cats." I rub the top of the kitten's head and it closes its eyes as though it's the best thing ever.

"Jesus, Twyla."

I give him my best innocent and hopeful expression. "Could it stay at your place overnight? I promise in the morning I'll call around and find a shelter, check if anyone has reported him or her missing."

"I don't know anything about cats."

I smile wide. "That's why I'm here. I'm a fountain of information. I worked at a pet store in high school."

He looks at me, then the cat, then back at me without saying a word.

"Please, Chase. We can't leave it out here alone to fend for itself. It's just a baby." I stick out my bottom lip, holding the cat out like Simba from *The Lion King*.

Chase pinches the bridge of his nose and sighs. "I'm

gonna regret this."

"I promise you won't. It's just one night."

He stares at me. "Is it gonna piss all over the place?"

I shake my head. "We can set up a litter box for it since I have stuff for Kiwi at my place, and you can keep it in your bathroom in case it does have an accident, but most cats catch on pretty quick how to use the litter."

"One night, Twyla." He holds up his pointer finger.

I do a little dance. "Thank you! You won't regret it, I promise."

"I promise you I will," he grumbles as we make our way toward the entrance to the building.

But I can take his grumbling if it means he'll give this little one a place to stay tonight. I wouldn't be able to sleep at the thought of leaving it out here on the streets.

On the ride up in the elevator, I fuss with the kitten while Chase watches me, not saying anything. As we start down the hall, I go through what needs to happen in my head.

"Do you have a casserole dish?" I ask him, and he gives me a look. "Right, of course you don't. I'll grab one from the condo I'm in. We can put a little bit of litter in there and use it as a makeshift litter tray. I'll buy him a new dish."

We both go to our apartments and I wait while Chase unlocks his door, then I hold the kitten out to him.

His eyes widen and his hands go up in front of him. "I'm not touching that thing."

I cock out a hip. "I could put it down, but it might get scared and burrow in under something where we can't get it. If that's the case, it could be days before it comes out."

A line forms between his eyebrows and he huffs out a sigh. "Fine." He holds his hands out to take it.

The kitten squirms, sick of being held out, and it's all I can do not to laugh when Chase holds it in front of him as though it's a bomb that could detonate with his slightest movement.

"Cradle it against your chest and pet its head. It seems to

like that." I give him an encouraging nod, like I might give the kids in my class when they're afraid of something.

He does as I say, and I wish I could snap a picture because seeing Chase carefully cradle this little orange piece of fluff is the kind of thing that gets a girl's ovaries going.

"I'll be right back. Leave your door open." I turn and open the door to the condo I'm staying in.

Kiwi is sleeping on the couch in the living room and doesn't give me more than a cursory glance. Once I've gathered up some food, kitty litter, and a casserole dish, I head across the hall to Chase's place. He's standing just inside the door, cringing while the kitten takes a stroll up his chest and across his shoulders.

"This little shit's claws are like needles," he complains.

It's true. I remember that from my time at the pet store, but it's still amusing to see a man who pummels and gets pummeled by two-hundred-something-pound men for a living complain about a little kitten's claws.

"Bring it to the bathroom." I carry all my supplies into the bathroom and set them down on the counter, then turn around. Chase comes through the door, and it's then that I realize how small the space feels when he's in it. "All right, close the door and I'll get it off you."

Chase closes the door at the same time as the kitten decides to take a route down his back, and a few unhappy grumbles slip out of Chase's mouth. Thank God he still has his tuxedo jacket on, otherwise it would be worse.

I gently pull the kitten up. At first it won't retract its claws, so it pulls at the tuxedo jacket, but the kitten finally relents. I set it on the floor, where it immediately gets to work sniffing everything.

"Can you grab two bowls from the kitchen? I'm going to use one for food and one for water."

Chase nods and leaves the room, probably happy to escape.

56

I set up the litter and set the furball inside to check it out. It's not ideal, but I think it will work. My instinct is proven right when it takes a small pee in the litter right away then covers it up.

The door opens behind me, and I turn with a big grin. "It just peed in the litter."

"Good. Here you go." He holds out two plain white bowls.

I fill one with water and the other with food. After a few cuddles with the kitten, while Chase watches, I stand to leave.

"Thanks again for doing this." I open the door and step into the hallway.

"You owe me." He closes the door behind us.

"I do. Your call. You just say the word and I'm all yours." I walk down the hall to see myself out.

A sort of strangled sound comes from Chase. I look at him over my shoulder, but he just keeps walking, following me to the door.

"What time do you leave in the morning?" I ask.

"I don't have to head out until a little later tomorrow because of the gala tonight."

"Okay if I swing by around nine then?"

"Yep."

"All right, see you then." He opens the door for me, and I step across the hall. I open my door and turn to look at him one last time. "Thanks again for tonight. For all of it."

Then I let the door close, pretending I didn't notice the soft expression that fell across Chase's face.

ten

. . .

Chase

I drop my bag on the floor by the door and head into the kitchen to make a smoothie. I'm not two feet into my apartment when a knock lands on my door, so I circle back around to answer it. I'm not sure why I didn't expect it to be Twyla.

"You look tired," Twyla says.

Normally I'd be fixated on her, but she has the cat in the carrier. The cat that was *supposed* to be dropped off at the shelter today. The damn cat meowed at the bathroom door all night and even closing my bedroom door didn't drown out its cries.

"Practice and a long, sleepless night will do that." I arch a brow.

A guilty look washes across her face. She looks down at the carrier and I already know I'm not going to like what's about to come out of her mouth.

"What's that thing doing here?" I step back to let her in.

"Well... funny story. When I went to the nearest shelter, they said they were full, so I thought it would be a good idea to have him checked out by a vet. You know, just so we'd know what we're dealing with."

I equal parts hate and love the "we" in that sentence.

"What did the vet say?" I'm only asking because I should, not because I actually care. It's obvious Twyla's already half in love with this little creature, but she's alone in that department.

"Vet says it's a Maine Coon, which seems fitting and he gave him all his shots." She bends at the waist and sets the carrier on the floor.

"Which means?"

"They're the biggest domesticated cats you can get, and we were the ones who found it and you're, well... big."

I hold back the flippant response on the tip of my tongue that I can show her just how big I am. "That still doesn't explain why you still have it."

"*He* has no place to go," she says. "All the shelters are full —I called around to a bunch of other ones in the area. And the nonprofit rescues I found aren't taking any more animals."

"That doesn't answer the question... what's *he* doing here?" I cross my arms and look down my nose at her because there's only one place this is going and I see a lot of sleepless nights in my future.

"Can he stay here a little longer? It will give me time to see if I can find a family to take him." She puts her hands up in a prayer pose. When I say nothing in response, she continues. "Please, Chase?"

Those two words in that sweet voice go straight to my dick.

She bends over and opens the carrier, pulling out the orange hairball. "If I leave him at the shelter, he's liable to be put down. Look at this sweet little face. Could you imagine? He's so little and hasn't been given a chance in this life."

I'm looking not at the cat but only at her. Those big, expressive eyes and the way they hold so much hope. How can I be the asshole who stomps all over that?

My teeth grind together as the realization that I'm going to have a furry houseguest for a while sets in. "Fine. But I get to name him while he's here."

She grins, eyes sparkling now, face full of sunshine. Putting that smile on her face is worth every irritation this cat will bring into my life.

"Deal."

I nod as though it's settled.

She cuddles the cat into her chest and suddenly I'm jealous of a fucking kitten. "What will you name him?"

I put my hands on my hips and give it some thought. "Not sure. It has to be something strong, tough."

She giggles. "What about Leo? You know, since he's orange like a lion."

I shake my head. "Too on the nose." I contemplate it for a beat and say the first name that pops in my head that doesn't sound froufrou. "Zeus."

"Like the god?"

"Yup. He was the top deity in ancient Greek mythology, the ruler and protector… it suits him."

She looks at the kitten with a smile. "I think it does too." Then she looks at me. "We should probably go to the pet store to get him some things since he's going to be staying here."

Twyla bites her plump bottom lip and I shift my stance so that she doesn't notice the half chub in my athletic pants.

"How much stuff does a little kitten need?" My forehead wrinkles.

"You'll be surprised."

"Fine. Let me make my smoothie first." I turn and head into the kitchen.

"Maybe I should go on my own. I'm the one who roped you into this. Technically, I'm responsible."

I reach the other side of the island and turn to face her, leaning with my palms on the counter. "Twyla, it's fine. Just give me a few minutes."

"Okay." She smiles with relief as though I made her day. "I'm going to go put Zeus back in the bathroom so he doesn't get into trouble while we're gone. We can let him explore once we get back."

She turns around and I watch her walk down the hallway. Only a small part of me is ashamed that I'm checking out her ass the entire time.

———

"So we're going to need a kitty litter pan, some kitty litter, food, treats, some toys, probably a brush, and a toothbrush and toothpaste."

"You're kidding, right? Toothbrush and toothpaste?" I stand with my arms crossed, looking down the cat aisle at the pet store. An aisle that is entirely too long with way too many products. People are psycho when it comes to their pets.

"No, you have to start brushing their teeth when they're little, otherwise they won't let you do it when they're older. Oral hygiene is important in animals too."

It's sort of cute how serious she is about it.

"Twyla, I am not brushing the cat's teeth."

She shrugs. "That's okay. I'll do it."

It shouldn't make me happy that she'll have to come over to my place to brush Zeus's teeth, but it does.

"Oh, and we'll need something to clip his claws." She walks down the aisle in search of the extensive list of things in her head.

Half an hour later, our cart is full as we push it up to the checkout. Twyla tries to skirt past me to the cash register, but I shift, blocking her way.

"I got it."

"No way. You didn't even want the cat in the first place." She moves to get around me, but I'm wide enough that I fill the tiny aisle between registers.

I gently place a hand on her shoulder. "It's not a big deal. You save your money."

Her cheeks pinken and I worry my words embarrassed her. Great. I'm trying to be a nice guy and I manage to come off like a jerk.

"Do you need some bags?" the teenage cashier asks.

I give Twyla a look, and with a small huff, she steps back.

I turn to face the cashier. "Yeah, we'll need some bags."

She rings everything through, but before she can tell me the total, someone hollers, "Andrews, good game last weekend!"

Twyla, the cashier, and I shift our attention to the end of the line, where a middle-aged man is smiling and giving me a thumbs-up.

I raise my chin. "Thanks, man." Then I return my attention to the cashier.

"You guys gonna kick Carolina's ass this weekend?" he says loudly enough that everyone at the other cash registers are turning to look.

"That's the idea." I turn my attention back to the cashier, wanting to get the hell out of here now before it becomes a whole thing. "How much is it?"

"Oh my god, Chase Andrews!"

I glance up as a little boy of about nine or so rushes away from his mom's side over to me.

"Ethan! Get back—" Her words die on her lips when she sees me. "My husband is gonna die when he finds out we met you."

My shoulders sink and I pull my wallet out of my pocket, handing the cashier my card. "Just put whatever it is on there."

By the time I'm done paying and we've packed the cart with our bags, a group of people are waiting near the exit for me.

"Sorry about this," I mutter to Twyla.

I sign all the random items they shove at me, take a few pictures, and have as little conversation as possible before Twyla and I finally head back to my truck. I open the back door and turn to get the bags out of the cart.

Twyla passes me one of the bags. "You seemed… I don't know, uncomfortable back there."

I take the handle of the plastic kitty litter container because Twyla could barely pull it off the shelf. Who knew the stuff cats shit in could be so heavy?

"I don't like the attention." I shrug and place it on the floor of the back seat.

Twyla chuckles. "Kind of hard when you're a professional football player."

I grab the last few bags. "I play football because I love it. I love the competition, the game, the entire sport. The attention is a negative side effect of living my dream, as far as I'm concerned." She reaches for the cart handle, but I get it first. "I'll bring this back in. You get in the truck."

She allows me to take the cart back with no argument, and when I climb in the truck, she's smiling at me. "Thanks again."

I start the truck and shift to face her. "If I'm going to do this, you have to stop thanking me every five minutes. I agreed. End of story."

"I promise I'll try." Her laugh is musical and it might be my new favorite song. "I just realized something while you were putting the cart away."

"What's that?" I put the truck in reverse and hook my arm around the back of Twyla's headrest, reversing out of the parking spot.

When she doesn't respond, I glance at her before putting the truck in drive and stepping on the gas. She's looking at me kind of funny.

"What's wrong?" I ask and glance at her again before I make a right.

She gives her head a shake. "Nothing."

"Bullshit. What is it?"

"It's embarrassing." She brings her hands to her face and covers it.

"Well now I'm gonna make you tell me." I'm curious what she would find so embarrassing.

With a huff, she drags her hands down. "Fine. I've just always thought it's sexy when a guy does that."

I frown. "When a guy does what?"

"You know." I glance over and she makes some gesture with her hands. "Puts their arm behind your headrest and reverses."

A deep chuckle rumbles in my chest. "Are you saying you think I'm sexy?" I'm not really a teasing kind of guy, but she's pulling it out of me.

"I said the act itself is sexy."

I bring the truck to a stop at an intersection. "Yeah, but it was so good when I did it that you were left speechless."

"Don't blame me. Blame the muscles." She crosses her arms in a huff.

"It's okay, I won't tell anyone you like my muscles." I glance over and elbow her.

She rolls her eyes good-naturedly. "Most people just use the cameras and don't even look behind them."

"Force of habit from old trucks in Montana, I guess." I shrug and ease the truck forward when the light changes.

"Anyway, like I was saying… the vet gave me a supplement to mix into the wet cat food three times a day because he's a little underweight, but you're going to be gone a lot of the time."

We round the street our condo is on, and I hit the button for the remote that controls the underground garage door. "I'll give you a key to my place and you can go in there and feed him."

"You'd do that?"

The surprise in her voice has me wanting to stop and look at her expression, but I can't look at her because I'm navigating the underground garage and it's always a tight squeeze for my truck.

"Of course, why wouldn't I?" I park in my designated spot.

"You're such a private person. I figured you wouldn't want a virtual stranger wandering around your place when you're away."

"A stranger, no. You, I'm fine with." I look over at her, a little startled when it dawns on me how true that statement is.

eleven

. . .

Twyla

The next day at lunch, I pop by Chase's place. After we set up everything in his place, he told me he would feed Zeus before he left for practice today, so I'm on the lunch shift. As soon as I step into his apartment, Zeus hops down from something in the kitchen and trots over to the door with a meow.

"Hello, cutie pie." I pick him up and tell him what a handsome boy he is as I walk through the living room and dining room toward the kitchen.

I put him down to grab his food, and he weaves between my legs while I prepare the plate with his food and the supplement. He pounces on the plate as soon as I put it on the floor.

"Must have been hungry, little guy," I say, putting away all the supplies.

Since I need to make sure he finishes it all, I check to see if the kitty litter needs to be changed. I'm sure Chase will be thankful for that. I walk down the hall and pass the spare room with the door that's locked.

Chase may not mind if I'm here when he's not, but he made it clear that I'm not to go in the room with the closed door. I have no idea what's behind that door, but the fact it's locked, plus he told me to stay away, piques my curiosity. Everything from an office with important documents to a secret sex lair has run through my brain.

When I reach the closet door that's been left ajar for Zeus to come and go, I swing it open and see that the litter is clean. What a surprise! Chase must have cleaned it before he left for practice.

Leaving the door open a crack, I head back to the kitchen. Zeus is just finishing his food, so I grab the comb from the cabinet Chase designated as Zeus's and sit on the floor beside him.

The minute the brush comes in contact with a snag, he meows and tries to run away, but after about ten minutes of stopping and starting, I offer him a few treats as a reward. Hopefully grooming is something he'll get more used to and he'll understand that when it's done, he gets a reward.

Then I hold him up near my face and take a selfie of the two of us. On impulse, I forward the picture to Chase. We exchanged numbers yesterday so that I could get a hold of him if there was any issue when I popped by his place.

> Me: Just brushed the big guy. Look how handsome!

Figuring it will be a while before I hear back from him, I throw out the fur that's in the brush, top off Zeus's water dish, and put the empty plate in the dishwasher.

I'm just saying my goodbye to Zeus when my phone buzzes in my back pocket.

> Chase: I thought I was the big guy.

He did not go there.

My cheeks heat to the same level they did last night when

67

I mentioned his muscles. I don't know what I was thinking. Maybe Chase's blunt-and-to-the-point personality is rubbing off on me. But it's hard not to notice his muscles. I mean, they're always *there*. They were present when we were dancing and my hand rested on his back, and I can't miss them in his tight football uniform. Not to mention the stretching T-shirt he wore last night.

I lock up the apartment and leave, trying to think of how to respond. His text was flirty and I feel as if how I answer will decide if I want to take our... relationship—no, friend-ship in that direction.

I'm still deciding when my phone buzzes in my hand. I look down, smiling and expecting to see something from Chase, but it's Mathew's name on my screen. Confusion swirls in my brain. Why would he be reaching out to me? I haven't spoken to him in months.

My thumb hovers over the notification while I contem-plate if I'm even interested in seeing what he has to say. After a minute of debate, I press on the screen.

> Mathew: For all your crying when we split, seems you moved on pretty quick.

Along with his message is a picture of Chase and me at the gala. It's the one the photographer took when we entered.

My first thought is how small I look next to Chase. My second thought is, what the hell gives Mathew the right to call me out? He's the one who told me he'd fallen in love with his coworker and that I'd practically pushed him to her because of all the wedding pressure. And he has the absolute audacity to scold me because it appears I've moved on?

> Me: It's not really your concern who I spend my time with anymore.

Even though I'm sure Mathew doesn't really care whether I've moved on, it's likely a sore spot that I was photographed with one of the Kingsmen players. He was always uncomfortable and insecure when I visited my brother because he knew I'd be around the guys on the team. He never wanted me to go and I never invited him because I knew how Miles felt about him—even if I didn't share that knowledge with Mathew. Having him tag along would have made for an awkward visit for everyone.

The three dots appear immediately.

> Mathew: Were you already hooking up with him when you'd visit Miles?

Tears spring to my eyes in a mix of frustration and anger. I shouldn't care what Mathew thinks. He made it clear he was finished with me. But there's a little inkling of hope somewhere in my mix of emotions, as though maybe he's asking because he does care on some level. And that makes me feel like a total loser because this man embarrassed me in front of both our families and friends, and he is so not worth my tears.

> Me: Why are you even texting me?

A minute goes by with nothing, so I set my phone on the counter and head into the living room where Kiwi is curled up on the couch. I lie down and cuddle her. She peeks open one eye to look at me, then closes it again and falls back to sleep.

I lie there for a while, thinking of the happy times with Mathew, until the memories end with the day he picked me up at my parents' house to go for a drive and told me he was calling the wedding off. At some point, I drift off.

———

A knock on the condo door wakes me. I bolt upright on the couch, startled. It hadn't been my intention to fall asleep. I was just feeling sorry for myself before plastering on a smile and carrying on with my day. The knock sounds again so I stand, rubbing my face to shake off the brain fog from being woken.

I don't even have the presence of mind to look through the peephole and see who it is before I open the door. Chase stands in the doorway wearing a different version of what he had on after practice yesterday—a pair of black athletic pants and a white T-shirt that hugs the muscles in his arms and chest in the most delicious way. God, he really is a gorgeous specimen.

He studies me for a beat, a crease between his eyebrows. "Figured I'd see how Zeus did today."

A yawn escapes me and I put my hand in front of my mouth. "Oh, yeah, he ate all his food, and he wasn't too terrible when I brushed him."

Chase doesn't say anything. He's staring at me, and I shift in place and look down. What is wrong with me? Eye boogers? Wrinkles from the couch pillow on my face?

"What's wrong?" His voice holds an edge that makes me feel protected.

"Nothing. What do you mean?" I straighten, locking eyes with him and smiling.

He shakes his head. "Nice try."

My shoulders slump. "Mathew texted me. He saw a picture of us together at the gala. He accused me of… hooking up with you when I was still with him." My cheeks heat at the admission because I'm sure Chase probably hooks up with Instagram model types, not mild-mannered teachers from the East Coast.

"That's none of his business." His hands fist at his sides.

"That was my response. Anyway, it kind of bummed me out. I'm making good progress moving on with my life and that brought it all back to the surface." I'm not sure what to do, so I continue standing in the doorway.

"Screw him. You don't owe him anything."

"I know."

He glances over my head into the condo, then his eyes fall down to mine. "I was just about to make myself dinner. Want to join me?"

I don't know if he's asking me out of pity or if he genuinely wants my company, but I smile. It will be good to get out of my own head. "That would be great, if you're sure."

He shrugs a big shoulder. "No sense in both of us eating alone."

It's not exactly a ringing endorsement that he wants me to be his guest of choice, but I'll take it because he's my guest of choice.

twelve

• • •

Chase

As soon as Twyla opened the door to her condo, I could tell she was upset. She put up a good front, but it was clear from the lost sparkle in her hazel eyes.

When she told me her ass of an ex had reached out to her, I wanted to demand that she give me his number so I could set him straight. I kept my caveman instincts in check because she's not mine. But my invite to dinner is because the thought of her alone in her apartment, moping, grates on me.

She said she wanted to change into something more comfortable, so I return to my apartment. Just like when I arrived here a half hour ago, Zeus trots over, tail straight up in the air, and rubs himself on my legs—leaving a trail of cat hair in his wake. My black athletic pants are full of hair now.

Ignoring the cat, I go into the kitchen to start dinner since I told Twyla to let herself in. I remove the salmon and vegeta bles from the fridge and get to chopping up the veggies.

About ten minutes later, the door of my condo opens and Twyla appears in the kitchen wearing a pair of high-waisted black leggings and a thin sweater that hangs off one shoulder. Her hair is in a messy bun on the top of her head. She looks cute and wholesome but somehow still sexy as hell.

Apparently that's a combination that does it for me because it takes a helluva lot of willpower to strip my eyes from her and concentrate on the veggies I'm cutting so I don't lose a finger.

"You like salmon?" I ask.

"Yeah."

I finish cutting the veggies, throw them in a bowl and add a little olive oil and seasoning, then mix it all together. I set them all on the metal grate I use on the barbeque to roast vegetables, then pull the cedar board I let soak in the sink all day out of the water.

Once I have everything ready to put on the barbeque, I look over to where Twyla is playing with Zeus with some string-on-a-stick toy she grabbed at the pet store.

"I'm just going out to the patio to grill."

She looks away from the cat, quickly standing. "I'll join you."

A sense of pride that she's choosing me over the damn cat washes over me, as absurd as that is.

She helps me carry the veggies out to the balcony. Once everything is grilling, I sit across from her at my outdoor table.

"Thanks for making me dinner," she says.

"You say thank you a lot, you know that?"

"What's wrong with that?" She pretends to be offended, but I don't think she really is.

"Just an observation."

"Tell me, what else have you observed?" She tilts her head and gives me a flirtatious smile. My dick perks up.

"That you don't text back."

The smile slips from her face. Shit, I ruined our moment.

"I was trying to think of something witty to respond with when Mathew texted and threw me for a loop. Then I lay down on the couch and fell asleep. I meant to text you back."

You, Chase, are an asshole. "I shouldn't have said anything."

73

I don't know why I got hurt when she didn't respond. Maybe because my guard's been slipping with her? Maybe what I really am is frustrated with myself because I checked my phone every five minutes after I sent that text to her.

"I like that you care if I respond," she says in a quiet voice, and we lock eyes.

I'm not sure what to make of her confession.

"I should check on the food." I stand abruptly and walk over to the grill, lifting the lid.

While I move the veggies around, I can't help but wonder what Miles would think if he knew she was here with me. Would he be pissed about it? Do I even care? I do on some level—he's my teammate and friend. It's bad for the locker room if I piss him off and we end up at odds. But he should see by now that Twyla is an adult and can make her own decisions. Besides, it's not like we're doing anything other than sharing a meal. It's not like her leggings are around her ankles and I have her bent over the balcony, drilling into her from behind.

Fuck. Now that visual will be stuck in my head for the rest of the night.

I finish what I'm doing and rejoin her at the table. She's staring out at my view of the city.

"Do you mind if I grab myself some water?" she asks.

"Shit. Sorry, I didn't even ask if you wanted a drink." I push away from the table while she stands.

"Sit. Relax, I can get it. You've worked hard all day and all I've done is hang out with cats." She chuckles. "Want anything?"

I shake my head. "I'm good."

She returns a few moments later and sits across from me with a bottle of water. I like that she's gotten comfortable in my space so quickly, but I'm not sure what that means either. Usually I hate people around my things. Even during poker nights, I hide shit and lock my bedroom door so nobody gets nosy.

"Can I ask you a question?"

"Of course." She unscrews the cap off the bottle.

"Why is Miles so overprotective of you?"

There's a slight dip to the smile on her face. She doesn't lose it totally, but it's obvious that whatever she's remembering isn't a good memory.

"You don't have to tell me if you don't want to."

She takes a small sip from her water and puts the cap back on. "You just caught me off guard. I can talk about it." She sits up a little straighter in her chair. "When I was seven, I got spinal meningitis. I was really sick, and at one point, the doctors told my parents they couldn't do much more for me and they'd just have to wait and see whether I was strong enough to fight through it with all the medications they'd already given me."

I clear my throat. "Shit, I'm sorry."

"Honestly, I don't remember a lot about when I was sick. But I know it was pretty hard for the rest of my family."

I nod. "It makes sense why they all look out for you so much."

She rolls her eyes playfully. "Yeah, I mean, that started it, but when I went back to school, a lot of the kids were mean to me. Pretended they didn't want to be near me because they were afraid they'd catch what I'd had."

I glower at her. "Are you serious?"

She nods and brings the bottle of water to her lips. "Yep. That's what really started my brother on his crusade to make sure no one ever makes me sad. I used to cry on the bus on the way home and after school. After a few times, he put the kids in their place by starting a fight. The kids ran away and he's been my protector ever since."

Now I understand why Miles is such a crazy big brother, protecting her at every turn. If I think back to how I felt an hour ago, wanting to rip her ex limb from limb just because he'd texted her, I don't know what I'd want to do to someone who was purposely cruel to her.

"Does it ever bother you how he acts?"

She moves her head from side to side. "Sometimes. Mostly I try to remember how lucky I am to have someone in my life who cares about me so much. Not everyone is lucky enough to have that."

Always glass half-full with this woman.

"It's good that you see it that way, I guess." I push back from the table to check on the food. "Five more minutes and we should be good to eat," I yell over my shoulder, but she's walking my way. "Sorry for screaming."

She waves me off. "Okay, I answered your question… can I ask you one?" The way she's twisting her bottom lip makes me think she's nervous to ask me whatever is on her mind.

I close the lid on the grill and turn around and face her. "Sure."

"What's in that locked bedroom?"

I push a hand through my hair and my lips form a thin line. I've never shown anyone what's behind that door. Not that it's a big deal; it's just… personal. And I don't get personal with many people.

Twyla must sense my hesitation because she raises both hands. "You don't have to tell me. I was just curious."

She really is a beautiful woman who always finds the best in any situation, and all my fear about opening myself to people disappears when it comes to her. She is way too kind of a person to make me feel stupid.

"Come." I spin around and turn down the temperature on the grill, then I motion with my hand for her to follow me.

Zeus follows behind to the hallway, and I stop outside of the closed door. "We need to keep him out."

Twyla's lips twist to the side. "Now I'm even more intrigued."

I swing the door open before I change my mind. Zeus makes a mad dash into the room, but I snatch him into my arms.

"Oh. My. God." Twyla steps inside, her head on a swivel as she inspects every corner of the room. "You're a closet nerd!" She turns back around to face me, and I scowl at her.

"I'm a jock, not a nerd."

She laughs. "No jocks have this many Legos."

I roll my eyes and set Zeus out in the hall, closing the door before he can sneak back in.

Inside this room is my prized Lego collection displayed on custom backlit glass cases and tables spread out throughout the room.

"This is really cool," Twyla says, walking farther into the room.

My shoulders relax from seeing her impressed at the models I've built.

"I grew up in the middle of nowhere. Spent most of my time outdoors, but when I was inside during the winter months, I enjoyed Legos. When I was younger, my dad helped me. It was kind of our thing." A bittersweet feeling washes over me. "I kept doing it even as I got older."

She steps over to the case that contains all the space-related sets I've built. "What do you like so much about it?"

I walk over to the table displaying the city set. "It gets me out of my head, kind of like football does for me. You're not thinking of anything but what you're doing at that moment. This relaxes me."

She turns and smiles before stepping over to the next case. "That makes sense. That's how I feel about reading. It takes me away from everything going on in my life and I can sink into someone else's story. And since I read romance, I know there's always going to be a happy ending."

There's a joke about happy endings somewhere in there,

but I keep my mouth shut so I don't make her uncomfortable. I watch her quietly examine each of the cases.

When she's done, she turns to me and asks, "Which one is your favorite?"

That's easy. I walk over to the far corner of the room and point at the castle-like structure at the top of the case. "This one here. Night Lord's Castle."

"What makes it so special?"

I know why she's asking. In a room full of some really impressive builds, this one is unassuming.

"This was the first set my dad and I ever built together. Not this exact set, but I was able to track down an unopened box from a collector."

Twyla's hand lands on my shoulder. "That's so sweet, Chase."

My muscle flexes under her palm and she pulls away. I miss the heat of her skin immediately.

She clears her throat. "I bet your dad is impressed with your collection now."

"I hope so. He passed when I was in college." Before she can respond, I head for the door. "We should eat."

I like having Twyla around. I enjoy her company. But I don't want our evening to take on a sour note by talking about my dad and the past.

thirteen

. . .

Twyla

I hang up the phone with a sigh. I still can't find a no-kill shelter to take Zeus off Chase's hands, and so far, the advertisement I put on the local pet finder site has only turned up a bunch of weirdos I would never allow to adopt Zeus.

I'm afraid that if I don't find somewhere for him to live soon, my little feline friend will wear out his welcome and Chase will get rid of him. Though something tells me he's not heartless, just has that gruff exterior.

My phone dings in my hand and I see a text from Bryce.

> Bryce: Tell your cranky doorman to let us up.
> We come bearing wine.

I chuckle and type a response.

> Me: Good wine or the cheap stuff?

> Bryce: Does it matter?

> Me: Good point. I'll call down now.

I call down and ask the concierge to let up Bryce and whoever she's with. This visit is unexpected but pleasant. I wasn't looking forward to an evening in on my own. I came to San Francisco specifically because I knew some people here, but so far, I've been sheltering myself away.

A couple of minutes later, I answer the knock on my door to find Bryce and Violet.

"Where's Shayna?" I step back to let them in the condo.

"She has to fly out for their game tomorrow, so she's MIA tonight."

I close the door and lead them into the kitchen to round up some wineglasses.

"But we're here because even though you're in town, you've been suspiciously quiet. We're worried." Bryce sets two bottles of wine on the counter.

"You guys don't need to worry about me." I find the wineglasses in one of the cupboards and set three on the counter, then grab the wine opener I saw in the cutlery drawer.

"I know how hard it can be to end an engagement," Violet says. She called off her nuptials with her ex after she found out he'd been cheating. And then she got together with Brady Banks, the best wide receiver in the league.

"It's certainly not for the faint of heart." I hand the wine opener to Bryce.

"I had my good days and my bad days. When we hadn't heard from you since the gala, we figured it was time for a girls' night," Violet says.

"And we're nosy and wanted to see what your place is like." Bryce pulls the cork from the wine bottle, then looks around. "Nice digs by the way."

I slide the wineglasses across the counter to her. "It's not my style, but there're certainly worse places."

"Sure beats my apartment." Bryce finishes pouring us each a glass of wine then lifts her glass for a toast. "To fresh starts. May they bring happy surprises."

We all clink and sip from our glasses.

"Let's go to the living room." I lead them into the room, and we all sit down.

Kiwi comes in to check out the new additions, and after a few minutes of the girls fawning over her, she settles in her cat bed in the corner.

I sip my wine and look at Violet. "I didn't get a chance to ask at the gala, but what are you doing about work now that you're living with Brady?"

Violet works as a nanny to high-end clients. In fact, she and Brady started up when she was a live-in nanny for his six-year-old son, Theo. Of course, they'd had an anonymous one-night stand previous to that, so that didn't hurt.

"I think I'm considered a kept woman now." She frowns.

Bryce leans back on the couch. "That sounds ideal to me."

Violet and I laugh.

"I'm not going to go live in someone else's house and help to raise their children when we have Theo, so I put in my notice. For the moment, I'm volunteering at Theo's school—helping with lunchroom supervision and in the classroom. It's nice to spend extra time with him and see him interact with all his classmates."

I longingly think back to my students. I miss teaching, but I know I made the right call coming out here to get distance from my life.

"But... that's kind of related to some other news I have to share," Violet says with a big grin and flips her long, dark hair behind her shoulder.

"Oooh, do tell." Bryce waggles her eyebrows.

"Brady and I talked at the gala about how eager we are to start our lives together and decided that we're going to try for a baby right away."

My mouth drops open. "Oh my gosh, that's awesome." I ignore the pinprick of jealousy in my heart. I had hoped to be making similar plans in the not-too-distant future with Mathew.

"Wow. Congrats," Bryce says. "What about the wedding?"

"We're going to get married as soon as the season is over. I don't want anything huge anyway, so it shouldn't take too much to plan it."

"That's really exciting. Congratulations." I smile, happy that she and Brady were able to sort out their issues and begin a life together.

"Thanks. Who knows how long it could take, right? So we figured we might as well get started on the fun part—trying."

We all dissolve into a fit of giggles like middle schoolers.

"God, don't remind me of what I'm missing." I groan and take another sip of wine.

"Need I remind you that you don't have to be missing anything? You're single now. You can do whatever you want." Bryce's eyes widen. "You should be out at the clubs."

I sigh. "I know. I've just always been a relationship kinda girl, you know? I've never hooked up with anyone I wasn't already in a relationship with."

"Jesus, girl, we gotta get you out more." Bryce shakes her head.

"I don't know if I could do it. I miss sex, that's for sure. But when it comes down to it, I don't know if I could sleep with a man knowing there's no future for us."

"Are you ready to get into another relationship?" Violet asks.

I shake my head. "No. Not yet."

Bryce shrugs. "Then it's the perfect time to hook up with someone."

She has a point, I guess.

I hem and haw, moving my head from side to side. "I don't know."

"You need to get out there though. Your rebound bang isn't just going to knock on your door." Bryce stands and refills her glass before walking over to us to refill ours as well.

A knock lands on the door as she puts the bottle down. All our eyes widen.

"Or is he?" Violet asks in a creepy voice.

I get up off the couch and head to the front door. I look through the peephole and my stomach flip-flops when I see Chase.

Pressing a hand to my belly, I open the door. "Hey."

"Hey," he says kind of shyly, as though he's nervous or something. "Wondered if you wanted to watch an episode of *American Horror Story*." He rubs his hand over the back of his neck and his gaze flits away from me and down to the floor.

The other night after we ate dinner, Chase asked me if I had already watched *American Horror Story*, season ten. Chase and I had discussed our appreciation of horror movies on one of my visits, so he already knew I was a fan. But I haven't watched the new season because Mathew wasn't a fan of anything horror, so I only watched that kind of thing when I was by myself.

Since he hasn't seen the season yet either, I suggested we watch it together. It was too late to start it the night of our dinner though, because he had to go to bed early. Tonight was supposed to be our first viewing party.

I like that he made the effort to come over to ask rather than texting like most people would.

"I totally would, but Bryce and Violet stopped by unexpectedly and we just opened a bottle of wine." I don't bother inviting him in. I know him well enough to know he has no interest in socializing in groups more than he has to, especially with a bunch of women.

"Oh sorry." He steps back and looks flustered, the tips of his ears growing pink. No way Chase Andrews is embarrassed, but I have to admit, it's kind of cute and endearing.

"Maybe we can do it after your game in a few days?"

"You're not coming?" I can't tell from his tone whether he views this as a good or a bad thing.

I shake my head. "No, I'm going to stay here. Plus, someone has to take care of Zeus while you're gone."

Chase pushes his hand through his hair. "Oh right. I'm not used to being responsible for anything other than myself."

"I made a bunch of calls today but didn't have any luck for somewhere he could go."

He nods. "All right. Keep me in the loop."

"I will."

"Well, I'll let you get back to it then." He turns to head across the hall to his door.

"Chase?"

He circles around to face me, hand on his condo door.

I want to thank him for thinking of me and trying to pull me out of even more solo time in my apartment, but instead, I say, "Good luck at your game."

"I don't need luck. I've got the muscles, remember?"

He flexes and I almost have to wipe drool from my chin. These little glimpses of a lighter-spirited version of Chase that I get from time to time only make me crave him more.

"That's right, blame the muscles. I forgot." I close the door and lean against it, smiling at the ceiling for a minute before joining the girls.

"Now I understand why you haven't reached out. You've been busy."

I whip my head toward Bryce, on her way to the powder room presumably.

My cheeks flush in embarrassment. "It's not like that." I walk past her to go back to the living room.

She calls out behind me, "Don't think we're not discussing this as soon as I return."

I chuckle and shake my head. Bryce must hurry because she's joining Violet and me less than a minute later.

"That was Chase at the door," she tells Violet with a smug smile that makes me roll my eyes. What are we, twelve?

"I told you it's not like that." I bury my smile in my wineglass.

"What's it like then?" Violet asks, her eyes pinging between Bryce and me.

So I explain to them about how we found Zeus when we returned from the gala and how I'm helping to take care of him when Chase is gone. When I mention that he invited me to stay for dinner the other night, their eyes light up.

"He's totally into you," Bryce says.

"One hundred percent," Violet agrees.

"Just because he's nice enough to feed me doesn't mean he likes me. He probably feels sorry for me more than anything. The woman who was dumped by her fiancé months before the wedding and ran from her small town to deal with it."

"I haven't known Chase that long, but from what Brady says, he doesn't really like anyone. I think the fact that he's inviting you over to spend more time with you says a lot." Violet give me an indulgent smile.

"Agreed." Bryce smacks her hand down on the leather seat cushion beside her. "It's all I can do to rip ten words out of the man's throat when I'm interviewing him for the paper. But you… he seems to *want* to talk to you."

Are they right? I grow elated with hope, but I don't want to get my hopes up if they're way off base.

Wait. Do I want something to happen between Chase and me?

"It doesn't matter anyway. Miles would kill me. And him." I polish off the wine in my glass in one hearty gulp.

Bryce waves off my concern. "Miles needs to worry about himself and his game. He's not your keeper, and besides, he never has to know."

"What is it with you and my brother? Why do you guys dislike each other so much?" I tilt my head and study her.

She shrugs. "We just don't see eye to eye on anything."

Her statement rings true, but I swear there's more to it.

"I agree with Bryce," Violet says. "Coming from someone with a family who loves to make their opinion on my choices known… it's your life. You have to do what you think is best for you. Like coming out here, for instance. If you think there could be something between the two of you, you should explore it."

I twist my lips while I consider what they're saying. "But I'm not ready for a relationship at this point. Plus, I'm going home in a couple of months."

"So it's a fling." Bryce's hands fly up at her sides. "You roll around in bed with him for a couple of months, get over your douche of an ex, and go home feeling better about yourself and your future."

In theory, that scenario all sounds great. Fun even. But when I think of the possibility of hooking up with Chase, there's still a lingering nervousness underneath all the lust.

"As you guys know, I've never had a one-night stand before," I admit to the women.

"Brady was my first." Violet raises her hands. "Just saying. Look how that turned out."

"It turned out pretty damn well." I chuckle. "I'll think about it." I stand from the couch and reach for my empty wineglass to get a refill. "I don't know if it's a good idea, but I promise I'll consider it. If not with Chase, then with somebody."

But I already know there's no one else, even some stranger I haven't met yet, that I'd want to have a fling with besides Chase.

fourteen

. . .

Chase

We suffered our first loss of the season yesterday, causing me to be in a shit mood. I'm not happy with how I played. Normally I'd head down to The Crooked Nail to relax with a beer, but Twyla and I have pseudo plans.

I'm not really sure if she's expecting us to get together to watch *American Horror Story* tonight or if she meant it in more general terms, as in "sometime this week," but the idea of abandoning her and being the one to leave her disappointed doesn't sit right with me. Picturing her sitting in that condo alone and sad, like the frown she sported when she left my bathroom during the engagement party, feels a lot like getting pummeled by one of my opponents.

So after I feed Zeus his dinner because this damn cat is all over me about eating—meowing constantly, weaving in and out of my feet like he's hoping to trip me, and butting his head against my legs—I head across the hall and knock on Twyla's door. Yeah, I could text her, but that seems so lazy and impersonal when she's two seconds away. Or maybe I'm more desperate to be in her presence than I realize. I'm scared it's the latter.

She swings the door open with a smile. "Hey! I'd ask how the game went, but I was watching." She frowns.

I palm the back of my neck. "Yeah, it was a shit game all around. Feel like watching *American Horror Story*? I could use the distraction."

Her features brighten. "Yeah, that'd be great."

She joins me straight away, locking her door. Of course, she piles a bunch of cuddles and attention onto Zeus when he greets her at the door.

"He sure loves you," I say.

"What's not to love?"

She snuggles her face into Zeus's neck, which is good. Otherwise, she'd see the look on my face that probably reads, "I could be such a simp for you."

I clear my throat. "You want a drink?"

She bends over to set the cat down and her shirt gapes, so I quickly head to the kitchen rather than allowing myself a cheap view. There's no question I'd like to see Twyla's tits, but not like a creeper.

"Just a water for me." She follows me.

I reach into the fridge and grab a bottled water for her, sliding it across the island to her.

"Thanks. Just so you know, I didn't have any luck finding somewhere for Zeus to go while you were gone, but I do have a lead on a family Carly down at the corner store knows, so I'll follow up on that tomorrow."

I stop with my water bottle held halfway to my lips. "You know the name of the girl who works at the corner store?"

She shrugs. "Sure. I'm in there a few times a week. Don't you know her name?"

I shake my head then take a sip of my water. "No. And I've been here five years."

Twyla gives me a cheeky grin. "Well, I guess I'm more social than you are."

I chuckle. "Tell me something I don't know." She stares at me, and I shift in place. "What?"

"You should do more of that." The look on her face is wistful.

"More of what?" I arch an eyebrow.

"Laughing."

I roll my eyes. "So how are you settling in? San Francisco starting to feel a little more like home?"

She sighs and sets her bottle on the counter, screwing the lid back on. "Yeah. I've always loved this area of the country. I spent my entire life in the same small town. I think maybe I didn't know how much I needed a change until I came here."

"What was the sigh about then?" I hold her gaze.

"You're way more observant than people think," she says. "It's kind of annoying."

"If you say so."

"I miss teaching. But that has less to do with Connecticut and more to do with how I spend my time and the connection I have with my students. And I miss my book club. That's about it." A small frown mars her features. That one negative facial expression feels like a knife to the chest.

Before I really consider it, I blurt, "I could be in your book club." My cheeks heat.

Her mouth drops open. "You'd do that? I mean, it's a *romance* book club."

Inside I cringe. But the urge to be the person to fix one of her problems is too strong to deny. "You've helped me out with the kitten. It's the least I can do."

She gives me a look I interpret as "don't be ridiculous." "To be fair, he's here because of me."

"Still, if you need someone to be in your club while you're here, I can."

She smiles wide and it feels like sunbeams on my face. "That's so sweet of you. Thank you! I'll pick a book and drop it off."

Embarrassed, I push a hand through my hair and look at my feet. "Don't think anyone's ever called me sweet before."

"Well then, they didn't really know you, I guess."

The way she says it as if it's a fact and there's no disputing it makes me believe that's really how she sees me. Which feels... odd and somewhat disconcerting, but... nice, maybe?

"So what does a book club involve exactly?" I motion for us to head into the living room and she follows.

"I'll pick the book, then we designate an amount of time to read it. Then we meet up to talk about it. Whoever picks the book usually runs the meeting and they come up with questions or topics relating to the book that they want to talk about."

"All right, I can handle that." I sit in my usual spot on the right side of the couch.

Twyla stops and sort of looks between the sectional and the chair that's off to one side, as if deciding where she should sit.

I motion to my left. "Sit on the couch. It looks straight on to the TV."

If she sits in the chair, she'll have to sit with her neck turned the entire time.

With a shy smile, she sits to my left. Not all the way over in the other corner, but splitting the difference.

I lean forward and grab the remote that controls the TV and the sound system off the table and set up the show.

"You ready for this?" I ask. I'm not sure what to expect from this season, but in general, this show is usually pretty fucked.

"Let's do it." She smiles as I press the play button.

I know she doesn't mean *it*, but my body doesn't get the memo because my dick twitches.

We get through the first episode and decide to watch another. I noticed that Twyla was pretty antsy during the first episode, shifting in her seat a lot and flinching whenever a jump scare came on.

At one point in the second episode, she yelps when something happens on-screen and I glance over. "I thought you liked horror stuff?"

She looks at me, teeth pressed into her bottom lip. "I do. It doesn't mean it doesn't scare the crap out of me though."

It's then I realize that her hands are shaking.

"Jesus, you're shaking, Twyla. Come here." I don't know why I do it, but I lean forward and get up onto my knees, then pull her into my lap and spread my legs, leaning back into the corner of the couch so she's nestled between my thighs.

I almost let her go when she stiffens, but she relaxes into my hold and lets her head rest back on my chest. The fresh scent of her shampoo—cucumbers, I think—wafts up to my nostrils and it's all I can do not to bury my nose in her curls.

This is trouble. I know it. And I'm sure Twyla must too, but as I wrap my arms around her, settle them on her stomach, and feel her relax, I can't muster up the energy to care.

Twyla is like the brightest star in the night sky—of course she commands my attention. Of course I'm attracted to her. And the urge to comfort and protect her feels impossible to ignore.

I don't know what this means, if anything at all, but I know it's what feels right in this moment.

We turn our attention toward the show again, but I have no idea what the hell is happening because I'm fixated on every point of contact between our bodies. And I'm concentrating really hard to prevent myself from getting a hard-on. The last thing I need her to think is that I'm some pervert.

Zeus meows somewhere on the floor and Twyla pats her lap. Like the stud he is, he settles on top of her. I swear he almost looks over her shoulder at me with a smug look like, "You wish you could be between her thighs, don't you?"

We finish the episode, and though no part of me wants to move from this current position, I have to get to bed. My days start early during the season and it's important to maintain my schedule so I don't get fatigued.

I click off the TV and we sit in the silence for a moment. I think we're both wondering what this means. We've clearly crossed a line, but what lies on the other side of it?

All words are stuck in my throat, so rather than addressing the neon-pink bedazzled elephant dancing in the middle of the room while wearing a thong, I say, "We'll have to watch the other episodes soon."

Twyla shifts Zeus off her lap and stands from the couch. "Definitely." She doesn't turn and look at me as she makes her way to the door. "You just let me know what time works for you."

The closer she gets to the door, the more I feel the need to say something, but I don't know what exactly. So I keep my mouth shut and she leaves, closing the door quietly.

I stand in place for a moment, staring at the door. Twyla either has to go back to being my teammate's little sister or become the woman I'm interested in.

Both options scare the shit out of me.

fifteen

. . .

Twyla

"All right. Don't be such a stranger." Miles pulls me into a hug that I return.

I met him for an early dinner down the street from my condo. "I'm not trying to be a stranger, I'm just trying not to be a bother. You're busy."

He pulls away, hands on my shoulders and looking down at me. "Never too busy for my little sis."

"Be that as it may, I'm not here to be a burden. You're in season. I know how it is."

He squeezes my shoulders and his hands drop. "You should come to more practices. You're coming to the game on Sunday, right?"

I nod. "I'll be there."

"Good stuff. Want me to drive you home?" He glances over my shoulder in the direction of my condo.

I shake my head. "I'll walk. It's a decent night."

He obviously doesn't like my answer because the corners of his lips press together, but he doesn't argue. "All right. Text me when you get home, okay?"

I roll my eyes. "I'm not texting you when I get home. It's

three blocks." I walk backward away from him. "Bye, big brother."

He pushes a hand through the curls on top of his head. "Be careful." He uses his dad voice.

Rather than respond, I turn and give him a wave.

It was good to see him. We had a nice dinner, even if I felt mildly guilty the entire time because of what happened with Chase when we were watching TV.

We still haven't talked about it. Things were weird when I left that night, but when I saw him a couple of nights later, we both seemed content to pretend it had never happened. And I'm still processing how I feel about that.

On the one hand, we're asking for trouble. On the other hand, I've never felt as safe as I did in his arms. I already knew I was attracted to him—I'm pretty sure most women who come in contact with him are—but that night reconfirmed to me that he makes me feel safe and protected. Truthfully, it wasn't even something I knew I wanted, but when he held me, I sucked up that feeling like a sponge.

I push those thoughts from my head. Chase hasn't made it a big deal, so why am I? I'm probably just reading into it. Still, that doesn't mean I haven't imagined—a thousand times between then and now—what it would feel like to belong to him.

My phone buzzes in my jacket and I pull it out, finding Violet's name across the screen. "Hey, how are you?"

"I'm good. You?"

I step around a woman pushing her stroller. "Just had a nice dinner with my brother. I'm headed back to the condo now."

"Oh nice. Well, the reason I'm calling is because I heard something when I was volunteering at Theo's school today that I thought you might be interested in."

I tilt my head. "What?"

"One of the moms who helps out all the time has to move

away suddenly because of her husband's job, and the school needs someone to monitor lunch for the second-grade class as well as help out in the classroom sometimes."

My hand flies to my chest. "Really? That would be amazing!" Excitement fizzes through me. I love being in San Francisco, but I'm sick of only talking to Kiwi.

"I got the feeling you missed being around kids the other night," she says warmly.

"I do. So much." I stop on the curb and wait for the light to turn.

"There's a police background check that has to be done and other paperwork, but it shouldn't be a big deal. I'll text you the address and the name of the person at the school to talk with."

"This is amazing. Thank you, Violet. I'll get in touch with them first thing tomorrow." The light changes and I walk across the street, feeling lighter and happier.

"And the bonus is that we'll get to see each other more."

"Definite bonus." I laugh. "I'm really excited. Thanks for thinking of me."

We chat for another couple minutes until Theo needs something from her and we hang up.

I'm brimming with excitement by the time I walk through the condo doors. I have to tell Chase. We were just discussing the other night how I missed teaching. This might not be the same thing, but I'll get to be back in a school and around children again.

We have plans to watch another episode of *American Horror Story* tonight. He texted me earlier and asked if I was down. Though I had a moment's hesitation after what happened the last time, I said yes.

I glance at the screen of my phone and see that I'm about twenty minutes early. When the elevator doors open on my floor, I make my way down the hall and stop at Chase's door.

Since I'm a little early, I knock, even though Chase told me to use my key whenever I come over.

Zeus meows from the other side of the door. When Chase doesn't answer after I knock a second time, I decide to use my key. Maybe Zeus hasn't been fed dinner yet because Chase is running late?

I go inside and set my purse down and remove the denim jacket I'm wearing since it was a little cool out tonight. When I'm done, Zeus walks toward the kitchen, looking for his dinner, but I hear my name from down the hall. Changing direction, much to Zeus's dismay, stink eye and all, I head down the hallway.

"Hey, yeah, it's just me," I call. "Sorry, I didn't know you were here because you didn't answer."

"Oh, Twyla."

My brow furrows at the tone of Chase's voice. It sounds as if he's in pain or something.

The door to the Lego room is closed and he's not in the second bath, so I venture toward the master bedroom at the end of the hall. I've never been in this room before and I feel a little uncomfortable stepping inside, but when I hear my name in that tone again, I can't not investigate. The shower is running and I second-guess myself, but then I picture Chase having slipped and hit his head, blood rushing into the drain with the water and I can't leave without making sure all is well.

The en suite door is ajar, and I call, "Chase?" as I step into the doorway.

I'm stunned into stillness. I can't move and I can't take my eyes off the sight in front of me.

Chase is in the shower, naked, with his head tilted back, eyes closed while he strokes himself. His muscled forearm flexes with the movement and I can't bring myself to look away. He's glorious. That's the only word to describe what

I'm looking at. His hard shaft is long and thick and in proportion with the rest of him.

As I'm examining his dick, I hear his sharp intake of air and my attention moves back to his face to see him staring at me in horror.

That breaks me out of my daze. "I'm sorry!" I whirl around and give him my back. "I didn't think you were home, and I was just going to feed Zeus and then I heard my name, and at first I thought you were calling me and then I thought maybe you'd hurt yourself or something."

He doesn't say anything at first. The pinkening of my cheeks morphs from arousal to almost painful levels of embarrassment.

Then his voice comes out raspy and he shocks me to my core. "Don't leave. Watch."

I slowly turn around, and once I'm facing him again, I soak in my fill of him. One hand still rests at the base of his cock. His gaze is intense and unmoving, and I imagine it's a lot like how he looks at the opposing players in the lineup.

"Are you sure?" I whisper.

He nods and starts stroking again. This time his gaze is on my face and unwavering.

Heat pools between my thighs, and I squeeze them together in an attempt at some relief.

"Go sit on the counter and spread your legs." His voice doesn't leave room for argument, not that there's an argument in me.

I hop up on the counter between the two sinks on the vanity. His attention follows me, narrowed in like a sniper's laser sight. The hand that's not stroking himself moves to cup his balls and a small moan escapes me. I lean back against the mirror and spread my legs. I'm wearing a maxi dress, so I know he can't see anything.

"Now pull your dress up to your waist." His chin tips up and he looks down his nose at me.

Zero part of me even thinks about denying his request. I do what he says, and the hand on his balls moves up to press against the glass separating us, almost as if he wishes he could bust through it and get to me. His other hand continues to stroke, and I lick my lips, wondering what he would feel like in my mouth.

"Now touch yourself," he says in a deep rumble that makes my clit pulse.

I bring my hand between my legs, lightly applying pressure to my clit over the thin fabric of my panties. After a few seconds, I slip my hand under the band of my panties and touch myself bare with a long, drawn-out sigh.

Chase's hand on the glass clenches into a fist and he picks up the speed he's stroking himself with.

"What are you thinking about? I want to know what's going on in that head of yours," I ask.

"You. Your lips wrapped around my cock and what that would feel like. My tongue between your legs. What it would feel like to sink into you… taste you."

My nipples peak and I press harder on my clit in an attempt to sate the lust. "Do you think about that stuff a lot?" My voice is breathy and wanton, sounding nothing like me.

"Every time I see you."

I moan. I can't help myself. "God, me too."

That undoes him. His eyes squeeze shut, and his head drops back as he strokes furiously. "Fuck, Twyla."

My name from his lips almost sends me over the edge. I arch my back with another moan.

"That's it, sunshine. Make yourself come for me."

It's the pet name that does it. I come with a cry, my body jerking as sensation after sensation pulses through me.

I sag against the mirror and watch as Chase's jaw tightens and his arm and ab muscles flex as he strokes in an uneven cadence. He hunches his back, leaning toward the glass with one palm supporting his weight, and he comes on a groan.

His seed streams out and washes down the drain with the water, leaving him panting and staring at the shower floor while he collects himself.

And now, for the first time since I stepped in here, I'm self-conscious and don't know what to do.

I could explain away Chase pulling me into his lap while we were watching TV. He was comforting me, not a huge deal —even if it felt like something more at the time. And even this... technically, we haven't touched each other or fooled around, so maybe there's still a way to go back to how things were before. Even if I have firsthand knowledge of the vein that runs up the underside of Chase's cock.

He raises his head, water dripping down his face, and our eyes meet and hold. The intensity in them hasn't lessened, even after his orgasm.

"I'm going to go feed Zeus." I hop off the counter and leave the en suite, cringing at myself.

By the time I've fed the cat and gotten a bottle of water for my suddenly dry throat, I feel a little more like myself. Or at least I think I do until Chase walks into the kitchen, hair still damp, dressed in a pair of shorts and a T-shirt.

I can barely look at him, so I pretend I'm really interested in supervising Zeus's meal.

"Twyla, we should—"

"We should get started on the episode so you can get to bed on time," I say, cutting him off. I can't bear to hear him say it was a mistake. I need to shore up my defenses before another man rejects me.

I look at him and his brown eyes burn with intensity, but he must see something on my face that tells him I'm not ready to have this conversation, so he nods. "Yeah. Sure."

I don't get to sit in the cradle of his arms this time, which is disappointing at first. But I remind myself that I came to San Francisco to make my life easier, not more difficult, and Chase Andrews and the word difficult go hand in hand.

sixteen

. . .

Chase

"Don't you think, Chase?"

My name is the only thing that draws me from my thoughts as the guys and I eat lunch at the training facility. "Huh?"

"If we run more blitzes, we'll have a better result on Sunday?" Miles asks.

It takes me a minute to gather my thoughts because the truth is, I was thinking about his little sister masturbating on my bathroom counter last night, something I'm pretty sure Miles wouldn't appreciate as much as I did.

Fuck, Twyla was so hot pleasuring herself. The wetness of her panties and her hand sliding down. I cannot get the visual out of my head and I came twice last night after she left. She's the proverbial innocent good girl, so seeing her desperate and giving herself what she needed was one hell of a turn-on.

"Where's your head been today?" Lee asks.

"Nowhere." I clear my throat and glance at Miles. "Didn't sleep well last night. I'm tired."

"Been meaning to ask you if you've seen any guys coming around my sister's place? I had dinner with her last night, and when I asked her if she'd met anyone since she's been out here, she got kind of cagey."

"You think she's seeing someone?" Brady asks and glances at me.

Shit. Does he know something? Did Twyla tell Violet and she told Brady?

Miles shrugs. "Not sure. But I got the definite feeling that something's up."

I clear my throat and shove another forkful of whitefish into my mouth.

"I'm sure if she was seeing someone, she'd tell you," Lee says.

"Not necessarily," Brady says. "Maybe she doesn't want the headache of Miles's interrogation."

Miles frowns. "I just want to make sure she's with someone who knows her value and treats her right."

"Nothing wrong with that," I say. Weirdly, Miles and I agree on that point.

I'm not the guy for Twyla, which is what makes what's been going on between us so conflicting. Twyla deserves some supersmart guy who works in finance and wears a suit to work. Not a guy who grew up in the middle of nowhere, scraped by in school, and has barely acceptable social skills because he doesn't like most people.

That woman blooms when she's around other people, and someone like me would only hold her back. Eventually she'd be unhappy and resent me. She should be with someone who doesn't have to be as selfish about his career as I do. Professional football takes a lot of work and commitment and there's a lot of travel involved. Sure, my career is destined to be over at a younger age than most, but even then, I hope to get on a team as a coach.

Point is, I can't make her happy long term, so what the hell am I doing messing around with her in the short term?

Especially when her brother is my friend and teammate and would literally cut off my nuts if he found out.

"See, Chase gets it." Miles motions across the table at me and I feel like an even bigger dirtbag.

My phone vibrates on the table, saving me from having to respond. I lean back and turn it over to see who it is. Thank God I purposely turned my phone face down on the lunch table in case Twyla called or texted me because it's her.

> Twyla: Good news. That lead Carly gave me came through. I talked to the mom and stopped by the house earlier to check it out. Zeus has a new home.

For some reason, even though that cat is a pain in my ass, my chest tightens at the thought of him no longer lounging around and spreading cat hair around my place. I type out my response.

> Me: You okay with that?

She responds immediately.

> Twyla: Kinda sad. I really love that guy.

I picture Twyla curled up on the couch at her place and frowning, and I want to fix it for her.

> Me: Want me to drop him off at his new home? Might be easier for you.

> Twyla: Would you really do that?

> Me: Of course. When do you have to bring him?

> Twyla: I said I'd do it tonight.

Me: Consider it done.

Twyla: You're the best. Thank you.

I don't know what this foreign feeling in my chest is, but it kind of reminds me of when I had a wing-eating contest with one of the linemen last year.

"Who are you texting, man?" Lee asks.

I set my phone face down on the table. "No one you know." The lie slips off my tongue easily and I shift the conversation to Sunday's game against Atlanta.

I'm not sure if I'm pleased or appalled by how easy it is to pretend I'm not the worst friend ever.

———

Twyla sits on the floor of my condo, cuddling Zeus with unshed tears. My chest aches and it has nothing to do with how many bench presses I did earlier today.

"I'm going to miss you." She kisses the top of his head, then presses her cheek there. She looks up at me. "He's gotten so big since he's been here."

I stare down at her, hands on my hips. "Yeah. I would've liked to see how big he ends up being." It's kind of cool having a big-ass cat.

"I made the family taking him promise to send me pictures from time to time, so I can forward them on to you if you want." She raises her eyebrows.

I nod. "Sure, you do that." I'm not sure I feel it necessary to keep up with the cat, but I'd be lying if I said I wouldn't mind keeping up with Twyla once she leaves.

She returns her attention to Zeus. "You be a good boy for your new owners, okay, buddy?" Then she sets him inside the carrier to her right.

Zeus meows as soon as she's closed the front of it, and I

swear he's looking at her like, "How could you do this to me?"

She stands then bends to lift the carrier, holding it out to me. "Well, I guess you should go."

I take the carrier. "You going to be okay?"

She sniffles and waves off my concern. "Of course. Sorry, I think I'm a little more emotional than normal this week."

"What's up?"

The corners of her lips tilt down. For a second, I think she might not tell me, but then it all comes bursting out like a cracked dam. "This weekend was supposed to be my wedding. It's just bringing up a lot of emotions. It's not that I wish I was still marrying Mathew, not after what happened, but it still makes me sad. Sad and feeling kind of like an idiot because how did I not see what was going on?"

I set the carrier on the floor and pull her into my chest. It's instinctual—Twyla's hurting, and I want to comfort her.

"Because you're a good person and would never do that to someone." I rub her back. "I'm sorry he hurt you." I attempt to keep my tone even, though the truth is I would love to rip her ex's larynx from his throat for putting Twyla through this.

She pulls away too soon, and I miss the feeling of her small frame pressed against my larger one. "You should go. Otherwise I'm going to beg you to keep him." She lets out a watery laugh and goes to open my condo door.

I follow with the cat carrier in hand. "You want to meet up once I'm back and watch an episode of our show?"

"Our show" slips out naturally, but she doesn't question it. She just smiles and nods. "Text me when you're back and I'll come over."

I nod and walk down the hall toward the elevator. I don't have to turn around to know that she watches us the entire time.

———

I pull up in front of the home in the Outer Sunset district and kill the engine of my truck. Zeus looks up at me with wide eyes in his carrier that sits on the passenger seat and meows.

"Looks like a decent place. You'll like it here, Zeus."

He meows again.

Though I'm right here and I should be eager to get rid of this furball that unexpectedly came into my life, something stops me from getting out of the truck. I picture Twyla saying goodbye to him and I remember how annoying yet amusing it was when Zeus inspected the inside of every bag or box I brought into the house. How after every shower, he wanted to lie down in the water left in the basin, then dripped water through my condo for the next ten minutes. Or how he'd sometimes hop up onto a table or counter and flick things off for no discernible reason.

I realize that kind of like Twyla, he's wormed his way into my heart, and I know what I have to do, damn it.

I start the truck and drive away, back to my place. Zeus, you've got a permanent home.

When I arrive at my building, I head back up to my condo and let Zeus out of the carrier. He takes a few steps out then turns and looks at me like, "What was the point of all that?" He flops down on his butt and licks his nuts.

Welcome home, I guess.

I pull my phone from my back pocket to text Twyla.

> Me: I'm back. Head over whenever.

I walk into the kitchen to grab us a couple of drinks and Zeus follows, likely hoping for some treats or a second dinner.

The condo door opens, and I call, "In the kitchen."

Her soft footsteps near the kitchen, and once she's within

view, looking a little more put together now, Zeus meows his hello to her and trots around the corner of the island.

She stops abruptly and her hands fly up to her mouth. "What is he doing here?" Her eyes search my face.

"I couldn't do it. I got all the way there and I just couldn't give him to someone else." My cheeks heat with embarrassment. Seriously, I'm a tough football player and this does not make me weak. I repeat the mantra.

I know in that moment that it doesn't matter how much of a pain in the ass Zeus ends up being. It'll be worth it just to see this expression on Twyla's face and know I'm the one who put it there.

"Oh my god." She rushes toward me and throws her hands around my waist, pressing her cheek to my chest. "You kept him."

I let one hand rest on the small of her back and thread the other one into her curls at the side of her head. When she draws back and tilts her head up to look at me, our eyes lock and the tension between us snaps tight.

We stare at each other for one beat, then two, then the pull to her becomes too much and I lower my lips to hers. She sighs into our kiss, spurring me on, letting me know she wants this. The first press of my lips to hers is a mixture of relief and escalation. Relief because I've wondered since I first met her years ago what it would feel like to kiss her. But now that I know, it only drives my fervor for her higher.

With the first brush of my tongue against the seam of her lips, her fingers dig into the muscles of my back and she opens to me. I devour her as if I can't get enough, and truth be told, I can't. I'm surrounded by her scent, the feel of her and my erection presses into her stomach. When she purposely pushes into it, the friction causes me to tighten my hand in her hair.

She moans into my mouth, and I capture the sound, swallowing it down. Even though I want her more than I've ever wanted anyone, I pull away and rest my forehead on hers. There's little doubt that if I picked her up right now and took her to my bed, she'd let me have her. But she has a lot going on in her head and could use the time to make sure she really wants to take this further.

We both catch our breath for a moment, then I say, "I take it you're not mad that I kept Zeus?"

She laughs and drops her head to my chest, shaking her head from side to side. "Not mad at all. I'll text the lady to let her know the change of plans."

"Sounds good. Now, let's go watch our show."

She pulls away and gives me a brilliant smile. "Our show. I like the sound of that." Her cheeks pinken with her words.

"Me too, sunshine."

We cuddle up on the couch with our cat and watch another episode, both of us seeming content to take this new layer to our relationship as it comes.

seventeen

. . .

Twyla

The day I've been dreading is finally here.

It's the day that was supposed to be my wedding day. I haven't told any of the girls, and when Miles called earlier today to ask if I wanted to go for dinner with him after he's done watching tape with the team, I told him I preferred to be alone. It took some convincing, but he eventually gave in.

Mathew and I would've been married by now. It's four o'clock and we were supposed to be married at one. Right now, we probably would have been having our pictures taken. Pictures I thought we'd be showing our grandchildren one day.

Kiwi is cuddled up with me on the couch while I stare at some home improvement show I haven't been paying any attention to when there's a knock on the door. Not in the mood for company and figuring it's probably my brother disregarding my request, I ignore it, but whoever it is knocks again. I blow out an annoyed breath and roll off the couch, getting an irritated yip from Kiwi for moving her out of her comfortable position.

I'm still wearing my pajamas from this morning as I whip

open the door without looking to see who it is, ready to cuss out Miles for not leaving me alone even though the concierge should stop him. But it's Chase standing there. I can't even muster up the ability to be embarrassed that he's witnessing the fact I'm still dressed in my pajamas and have clearly done nothing with myself today.

"Hey," I say.

Even in my current state of mind, my lips tingle in remembrance of our kiss the other night. It was all-consuming and no part of me wanted to end things there, but I could tell Chase was trying to be respectful, even if his erection was pressed into my stomach.

"Hey. How are you?" He pushes past me into the condo.

I let the door close and turn to face him, trying to muster up a smile. "I'm good."

He frowns. "I know what today is."

I brush past him into the living room and lie down on the couch. "Yeah, what about it?"

He steps into the room and looks down at me from the side of the couch, hands on his waist. "How are you? It must be a hard day for you."

I shrug. "Kind of. But I'll be all right."

Chase blows out an annoyed breath. "Stop pretending everything is all right. It's okay to be pissed off or upset. You might be full of sunshine, but you don't have to shine all the time like the actual goddamn sun."

I slowly sit up, eyes narrowed. "I'm not pretending anything."

He scoffs. "Bullshit."

My mouth presses into a thin line for a beat before I can say anything, then I throw my hands in the air. "Okay, today sucks! Is that what you want to hear? All I can think about is what I should have been doing today. Then I feel sorry for myself, even if I don't want Mathew back in my life. It's confusing and sad and pisses me off that I still feel anything about it. Is that what you want to hear?"

The tiniest of smiles breaks through his stern features. "Exactly what I was hoping to hear. Now go get dressed, we're going out."

I blink a couple of times. "Excuse me?"

"Remember that day you saw me leaving the building and you asked where I was going and I didn't respond?"

I nod.

"Well, I'm going to show you. C'mon."

The urge to argue is there, but Chase is dangling the carrot of letting me in and showing me a side of himself I'm guessing not a lot of people know about. It's too tempting to ignore.

I trudge off to my room with a "Fine" and change into a pair of jeans and a fitted black long-sleeve shirt that hugs me in the perfect way. Then I throw my messy curls up into a ponytail, brush my teeth, and put on some mascara.

When I return, Chase is waiting at the door, scrolling through his phone. His eyes look up though his head doesn't move. "Ready?"

I nod, even though I have no idea where we're going. But he's wearing jeans and an olive-green Henley, so I figure my outfit fits.

He leads me out of the condo building and we walk down the street in the opposite direction of the restaurant I ate at the other night with my brother. We're quiet on our walk. Chase keeps his chin tilted down, but I notice a few people doing double takes as we pass. Chase doesn't alter his stride. Even if he is trying to keep a low profile, he's a big guy. He's hard to miss.

After less than a ten-minute walk, he stops in front of a dive bar with a weathered sign over the door that says The Crooked Nail.

"This is where we're going?" I ask, trying to peek through

the windows. They're dark and dingy, so it's hard to see inside.

He turns to look at me. "Yup."

Chase holds the door open for me. When we go inside, I'm immediately hit with the smell of stale beer. Though no one is smoking in there now, it has the distinct scent of people smoking in there for many years.

The floor is a beaten and battered wide-plank wood, and a pair of pool tables and darts are at the very back of the room. Circular four-seater tables dot the floor, and to our right is an L-shaped bar with a brass rail. On the walls are beer and alcohol ads from yesteryear, faded with the patina of time and the odd neon sign for different brands of beer and local teams.

It's clearly the type of establishment where regulars hang out. Everyone in the place—a grand total of maybe seven people—turns in unison to look at where we stand in the doorway.

"Chase, how's it goin', man?" the old guy behind the bar with a four-inch gray-and-white beard calls.

"Hey, Randy." Chase raises his hand in greeting and walks over, so I follow him. "I'll have my usual." He leans on the bar, looking more at home here than I've seen him look thus far in any environment, and looks at me. "What do you want to drink?"

"Um…" I glance at all the bottles lined up like bowling pins behind the bar and my gaze snags on the label with a pirate. "I'll have a rum and Coke, please." I don't bother asking whether or not I can get a glass of wine. It's very clear this is a no-wine establishment.

"Comin' right up," Randy says.

As he works on our drinks, Chase turns his attention to a man who looks to be in his midfifties, halfway down the bar to his right. "How's things, Phil?"

The man looks at him and shakes his head. "I'm trying, I'm trying. Just easier said than done."

"Don't forget, I can give you some tips if you need them. Just holler."

He nods in a way that makes me think Chase has made this offer—whatever it's about—before. "Will do."

"Here ya are." Randy slides my drink and Chase's beer over to us.

"Just add it to my tab," Chase says, picking up his beer and nodding in thanks. Then he leans in over the counter and Randy does the same. "Add whatever Phil owes to my tab too, okay?"

Randy nods and claps him on the shoulder for a beat before straightening. "Enjoy. Let me know if you need another round."

Chase nods and leads me to a table closer to the back, near the pool tables. Once we're seated, he says to me, "Phil was diagnosed with diabetes a couple of months ago and is supposed to be getting his diet and exercise together. I've offered to give him some eating or exercise tips, but he's not interested."

"I guess you can only lead the horse to water." I bring my glass to my lips and take a sip, making a face when I swallow.

"You don't like it?" There's a crease between Chase's eyebrows.

"No, it's fine, it's just strong. I don't drink hard liquor a lot. I'm a bit of a lightweight."

He chuckles.

"So what is this place?" I ask.

"What do you mean?" He looks around the place. "It's a dive bar."

I tilt my head and spear him with a look. "But what is it to you?"

He holds my gaze and blows out a breath. "It's the one

place in this city that reminds me of home. Reminds me of my dad."

I remember that his dad died while Chase was in college, but he's never said much else about him. I'll get to that, but first I want to know something else. "Do they know who you are? No one made a fuss."

He pulls from his beer and sets it on the table. "Why do you think I like coming here? No one treats me special, no one bothers me about my job… I just get to be Chase Andrews, guy who was raised in butt-fuck nowhere, not Chase Andrews, tight end for the Kingsmen."

I think back to how uncomfortable he was at the pet store that time all those people approached him, and I understand a little better why he likes it here, where no one treats him like he's a big deal. I take a sip of my drink, happy to be thinking of something besides feeling sorry for myself. "You said it reminds you of your dad. How come?"

He contemplates my question for a moment, and I sit in the comfortable silence, waiting patiently.

"My dad was a simple man. Salt-of-the-earth kind of guy. Ran our sheep farm until the day he died. There was this dive bar he'd go to every Saturday night. The first couple of years, when I'd return home from college to visit, he let me tag along even though I wasn't of age. Some locals ran the bar, and they looked the other way. Some of my best times with my dad were at that bar. He'd talk about life and what mattered most… he was a smart man." Chase stares at his beer bottle for a beat and I sense that he's reliving some memory of him with his dad. "Anyway, I feel close to him here. Feels more like home than the rest of the city."

"You don't like living in a city?" I ask.

He shrugs. "I don't hate it, don't get me wrong. But I never quite feel like I belong."

I nod, understanding what he means. "How did… I mean, how did your dad…"

"Heart attack." He frowns. "He'd been complaining about some symptoms to my mom for a couple weeks before it happened but wouldn't go see the doctor even after my mom got on his ass about it."

I reach across the table and squeeze his hand. "I'm sorry. That must have been awful."

He nods slowly and squeezes my hand back. "Yeah. At least football season was over because I was a mess and in my head the rest of that year."

His father's death clearly still affects him. I can hear the pain in his voice when he talks about his loss.

"Is your mom still on the ranch?"

He shakes his head. "She sold it shortly after my dad died to a neighbor who'd been eyeing the land, then moved back to Wyoming to be closer to her sisters. She's remarried now."

I don't sense any bitterness from him over the fact that his mom moved on with her life. That's probably the healthy response, but I'm not sure how I'd feel in the same situation.

Now that I realize exactly what this place means to him, my chest warms over the fact that he's sharing this part of himself with me. "Thank you for bringing me here and trusting me."

"You don't have to thank me, sunshine." He takes a pull from his beer and holds my gaze.

God, I love it when he calls me that.

"Today was harder than I thought it would be." I take a large sip from my drink, opting to open up and tell him how I'm feeling since he's done the same for me. "I knew today was coming obviously, but I thought I was prepared for whatever I'd feel today."

"I'm sure it's a lot." His mouth forms a thin line.

"I'm most annoyed that I still care, you know? I mean, it's not like I want Mathew back or anything."

"I'm glad to hear that."

"You are?" Even I can hear the hope in my voice.

He nods. "You deserve someone better than a guy who will do what he did to you."

I temper my disappointment by taking another sip of my drink. I guess I was hoping Chase would say he was glad because he wanted me and didn't want me with anyone else. We still haven't discussed what any of the stuff we've been doing means, and I'm afraid to bring it up because maybe I won't like the answer. Maybe he'll tell me it was a mistake, then I'll feel the same sting of rejection I did when Mathew broke things off.

I clear my throat. "Right. Maybe it's more about me mourning the life I thought I was going to have than it is about him. I figured I'd have started a family by the time I was thirty and that we'd have bought a house and all the stuff that comes with that."

Chase scoffs. "You're still young, Twyla. You're not thirty for what, another five years?"

"Sure, but it takes time to meet someone special, date them, and decide you want to spend your life with them."

He chuckles. "Not if you're Brady and Violet."

I smile. "True." I take another sip of my drink. "Where are the restrooms?"

He turns and points toward the corner of the room on his right side. "Down that hallway."

"Okay, I'll be right back."

I push out my chair and walk over to where Chase directed me. My phone buzzes in my back pocket and I pull it out as I'm pushing through the ladies' room door. Mathew's name is on the screen and I still immediately.

What the hell is he doing calling me today of all days?

My thumb hovers over the red X, but something in me won't let me press it. For some reason, I want to hear whatever lame thing he has to say. Before I can think too hard about my decision, I click on the check mark and bring the phone to my ear, but I don't say anything.

After a few seconds of silence, he says, "Twyla? I didn't think you'd answer."

"I wasn't going to. Why are you calling?" I step farther into the two-stall bathroom.

"You know what today is."

I lean my butt against the sink that's seen better days. "Exactly. So why are you calling?"

"I thought maybe you were feeling the same way I am today." He sighs.

"Which is how, Mathew?"

"Full of regret."

That surprises me, and I blink a few times. "At this moment, I'm a little more full of rage than anything."

"I know I messed up. I'm sorry I hurt you."

I scoff. I can't help it. "Seriously? You call off our engagement because you say you fell in love with someone else, yet you're calling me on the day that would have been our wedding and making it sound like you made a mistake?"

"I think maybe I did make a mistake."

I can picture him pulling on his hair the way he always did whenever he was stressed.

"You are unbelievable." I hit End on the call and put my phone on Do Not Disturb. "Unreal!" I shout into the empty bathroom before heading into the stall to do my business.

By the time I emerge to wash my hands, I'm incensed. How dare he? Did he call today because he thought I might be at my weakest? Well screw him.

Angry and agitated, I head out of the bathroom, determined to have a good time tonight and remove all thoughts of my loser ex from my mind.

When I reenter the bar area, I see that a group of three guys has entered the bar in my absence. They're at a table closer to the front of the bar, but they're making a lot of noise and are a lot rowdier than anyone else.

I walk over to the end of the bar and get Randy's attention. "I'll have another rum and Coke, please."

"Sure thing, sweetheart. I'll bring it over to you after I fix up these guys' drinks." He nods toward the noisy table.

"Great, thanks." I stomp back over to the table where Chase sits and flop down into my seat.

He eyes me warily. "Everything okay?"

"Yup, perfect." I bring my glass to my lips and tip it back, finishing it off with one gulp. "How are you at playing pool?"

Time to get this party started.

eighteen

. . .

Chase

I don't know what happened in that bathroom, but something sure as hell did because Twyla came out in a fiery mood and now she's on her fourth drink of the night. We played pool and darts for a while, and now we're back at the table. Twyla's hand is pressed to her cheek, elbow on the table as she leans in and stares at me with glassy eyes.

"Aren't there some rules for you guys the night before a game?" she asks.

I shrug. "It's fine. Worst that'll happen is I'll get a fine if they find out. Besides, I only had one beer."

There's no way I would get drunk the night before a game or be so out of it that I couldn't look out for her. Twyla clearly needed to blow steam off tonight and I'm happy to be the one she does it with. Or maybe I demanded I be the one she did it with. Semantics.

"Isn't it past your bedtime?" she says in a teasing voice.

"You let me worry about my bedtime."

"Why do you call me sunshine?"

I can see we're at the portion of the evening where she's drunk enough to blurt out any thought that comes into her head.

I could lie, but I'm not even sure she'll remember this tomorrow, so I decide to be honest. "Because you're like the sun—you bring life to anything you give your attention to. People open up, want more of you, like flowers turning toward the sun for sunlight. Plus, you have this annoying habit of always looking at the positive side of things."

She smiles at me, and her eyes look watery all of a sudden. "That's the sweetest thing anyone has ever said to me."

My cheeks heat in embarrassment. God, I hope she doesn't remember this in the morning.

She brings her glass to her lips and takes a big gulp. "I'm going to go to the bathroom." When she stands, she's a little unsteady for a minute but finds her balance.

"Maybe we should get going."

Twyla scoffs. "The night is young, big guy." She smacks me on the shoulder as she passes by.

I watch the three guys who are playing pool at one of the pool tables. They came in earlier and have been getting drunker and drunker as the night rolls on. So far they've seemed harmless, but they're loud and boisterous and annoying as fuck.

Twyla hasn't returned to the table after a few minutes and I'm about to get up and check that everything is okay when I hear one of the guys from the pool table say, "Hey, baby, why don't you come play with us? I can show you how to hold a stick." The innuendo in his voice is obvious and my blood runs cold as I slowly shift in my seat so I can see them.

Twyla is at the other pool table with a cue in her hand. "I'm going to play with my friend, thanks."

"Aw come on. Let the three of us show you how much fun we could all have together."

I push my chair out from the table to intervene, hoping that my presence alone will do the trick before this situation escalates. But when he reaches for her and pulls her into him by the waist, pressing his body to hers while she leans away, I see red. Adrenaline rushes into my system and every muscle in my body tightens, primed to do battle.

"Hey, man, the lady said she's not interested. Take a hike." I remove his hand from around Twyla and push him so he stumbles back a few steps.

"What the fuck do you think you're doing, huh?" He steps forward and I shift to stand directly in front of Twyla.

"Teaching you some manners, asshole." I look down my nose at him since he's shorter than me, hoping he'll do the smart thing and back the fuck up.

"Why don't you mind your own business?" he says, taking another step forward.

This guy doesn't know what's good for him.

"She *is* my business."

"Don't see a ring on her finger. We were just chatting." He pushes my shoulder, but I don't move at all. That's when his two friends come to stand on either side of him.

Without turning away from them, I say, "Twyla, go back to the table."

"But—"

"Table, Twyla. Now."

I hear her walk away, and that's when I step forward so I'm chest to face with the guy. "Next time you talk to a lady, do it with some respect. We're leaving now, but don't let me see your face in here again or we're going to have a problem. Got it?" I arch an eyebrow.

He scoffs but doesn't say anything, so I step back and turn to make my way to where Twyla is standing beside the table. Her eyes go wide. Next thing I know, someone jumps on my back.

Jesus Christ.

I bend at the waist and flip him over my head so he lands with a crash on the floor. When I spin around, one of the friends has his fist cocked, but I catch it with my left hand and use my right hand to punch him in the face. He wobbles back a few steps and crashes against a table, tipping it over.

The other friend comes running at me like a linebacker. I meet him halfway, tossing him onto the pool table.

I turn to make my way back to Twyla and the first guy I got into it with is wobbling to his feet.

I point at him and shout, "Stay down."

He thinks better of getting up and stays where he is.

Twyla's looking at me with wide eyes and disbelief. I don't know what comes over me, but when I reach her, I toss her over my shoulder before walking toward the door.

"Sorry for the mess, Randy. Send me the bill."

He nods and waves me off.

I'm not worried about this coming back to bite me in the ass. Everyone else here are regulars and will cover for me. Even if it did come back to haunt me though, it would have been worth it to keep Twyla safe from pieces of shit like that.

Once we're out on the sidewalk, Twyla asks, "Chase, why are you carrying me?"

It's dark now, but we've caught the attention of a few people.

"I don't know," I answer honestly.

"Can you put me down? I'm getting dizzy."

Shit. I gently bend and set her on her feet, gripping her waist to make sure she's steady on her feet before I let go.

"Sorry," I mumble.

"Don't be." She's looking up at me in something like drunken awe. "I know I shouldn't like it, but that was all kinds of hot, having you go all alpha male protective mode for me."

I chuckle. "Is that what that was?" I thought it was good old-fashioned jealousy.

"And then you just threw me over your shoulder. Definitely hot."

"Blame the muscles." I give her a wink at her inside joke and take her hand. "C'mon. I don't think those guys will try to follow us and come looking for more trouble, but let's get out of here."

She lets me lead her home, never dropping my hand until we get into the elevator. There, Twyla presses her body against mine, winding her arms around my neck.

"What are you doing?"

"Showing you how hot that was." She rises on her tiptoes and moves in to kiss me, but I pull away.

She frowns. "What's wrong?"

"Nothing." The elevator dings and the doors slide open, and I step out of the elevator. "How do you feel about sleeping at my place tonight?" I want to make sure she isn't sick overnight since she's had a lot to drink.

"I was hoping you'd ask." There's no mistaking from her tone that she thinks I'm asking her to stay for less-gentlemanly reasons.

We reach my condo and I get us inside, locking the door behind us. Zeus rushes up to say hello, and Twyla scoops him up and follows me down the hall to my bedroom, whispering praise to him the entire time. Once we're inside my room, she sets him on the bed and, without hesitation, whips off her shirt, leaving her in a sheer black bra.

My dick instantly twitches, and I use all my willpower to look away. I walk over to my dresser to find something for her to wear to bed and settle on one of my Kingsmen T-shirts. When I turn back around, she's already removed her shoes and socks and her jeans are halfway down her legs.

"Here, you can wear this." I toss it onto the corner of the bed, not wanting to get any closer to her, afraid my self-control isn't strong enough.

Her forehead wrinkles. "Why are you giving me clothes to put on? I'm trying to take them off."

"I see that. But you need to wear something to bed."

She finishes removing her jeans, then walks toward me in

her sheer black bra and matching panties. I know for certain this image will repeat in my brain for days. Weeks even. Maybe months.

"Chase, I want to be with you." She wraps her arms around my waist and rests her chin on my chest, looking up at me.

"I want that too, believe me. But now's not the time." I weave my hands into the hair on either side of her face and bend to give her a chaste kiss.

She frowns when I pull away. "Now is the perfect time." The little minx rubs her belly against my rock-hard erection, eliciting a low rumble from my chest.

"It's really not."

"Tell me why you won't sleep with me tonight. Why isn't this the perfect time?" Her voice sounds agitated.

"I don't want to be a regret, sunshine." I kiss her forehead. "You've had a lot to drink tonight, and if and when this happens, I need to know that you made the decision with a clear head."

"Oh, it's happening, big guy. You can count on that." Then she yawns and her eyes water.

I chuckle. "Put the shirt on and we can discuss this tomorrow."

She gives me a cute frown, then turns to grab the T-shirt off the bed. I have to adjust the hard-on in my pants at the view of her bare ass. I now realize she's wearing a thong.

Once she slips into my bed—and holy hell does she look good there—I pull off my own shirt, then remove my shoes, socks, and jeans. I step into my walk-in closet where my lounge pants are and slide on a pair before returning to the bedroom.

Zeus, that little shit, is lying in the middle of the bed, cuddled up to her side.

I turn off the light and slip under the covers, doing my

best to think of anything other than the fact that a partially naked Twyla is only a couple feet to my right.

After a minute or so, her soft voice cuts through the darkness. "Thank you for tonight, Chase. You made my shitty day much better."

"You're welcome, sunshine."

Then her breath draws evenly, and I drift off not long after her.

I didn't expect to end up in bed with her tonight, but I'm not complaining.

nineteen

. . .

Twyla

Heat presses into my back through the blanket and I slowly open my eyes. It takes me a moment to remember where I am and why.

The bar last night... having fun with Chase... those drunk losers who tried to hit on me... Chase showing them who's boss and throwing me over his shoulder, all caveman-like. It was so hot.

I grin and roll over, expecting to find Chase there, but I only find an annoyed Zeus, who's put out by the fact that I almost rolled onto him. With a frown, I glance around the room and don't see Chase anywhere. I don't hear the shower going either. Damn.

It would have been fun to join him, especially after he shut me down last night. Cause I'm not drunk now.

I sit up, and that's when I notice a note on his pillow. I pick it up, studying the masculine scrawl.

Left some ibuprofen and water for you. Lock up whenever you leave. See you after the game.

Chase

I don't know what to make of his note. It's sweet that he left me water and painkillers, but the note is generic and could have been left for anyone. There's certainly nothing romantic about it.

Maybe I came on too strong last night. Maybe drunk Twyla was too much for him. Chase doesn't like drama, and getting into a bar fight with three guys in the place he goes to find peace definitely counts as drama.

Shit. I owe him an apology.

The ibuprofen and water are on the bedside table on my side. I slug them back because I do have a dull headache that I know from experience will only get worse if I don't tend to it. Then I get out of bed and find my phone near my jeans on the floor, where it probably fell out of my back pocket.

It's 10:13 a.m., which explains where Chase is. He'll already be at the stadium.

Unsure whether I'm dreading or looking forward to seeing Chase, I make sure Zeus has food and water before I return to my apartment to get ready. I have to get a move on if I'm going to make kickoff.

———

I end up arriving ten minutes into the first quarter, after picking up the ticket my brother left for me at will call. I'm seated with some of the other wives and girlfriends of team members and make small talk with the ones I recognize before excusing myself to go to the concession stand.

My phone buzzes, and I pull it out to find a text from Violet.

> Violet: Are you here at the game? I'm in the
> owner's box with Theo and Brady's parents if
> you want to join us.

She's sweet for thinking of me. Normally I would join her, but after last night, I kind of prefer to sit with the women I don't know as well and keep to myself. Violet will probably be able to tell that I'm a riot of emotions as soon as she sees me, and she'll want to know what's up.

> Me: I'm here! Thanks so much but I think I'll
> stay down here in the action today. I'll see
> you after though!

> Violet: All right. See you then.

My brother left me a pass that will get me past security so I can see him and the guys afterward. He mentioned that some of them might go out and celebrate with a nice steak dinner if they win, and of course I'm hoping that will include Chase.

If my drunken memories are to be believed, something shifted last night, and I'm no longer content to wait and see what happens.

I grab my popcorn and drink and head back to my seat. Chase is on the field, looking fierce in his football gear, and I cannot take my eyes off him the entire game. It's as though my brain is primed to find number seventeen on the field or the sidelines, no matter what.

Maybe it's time to face the fact that I have it bad for the man and stop pretending otherwise.

———

When the game is over and some of the fans have cleared out, I head past security to wait by the locker rooms for my brother and his friends. I've just walked past the pressroom where the players and coaches do their after-game interviews when I hear my name. I turn to find a freshly showered Chase exiting the pressroom. He must have just finished his interview.

"Hey." I smile, but I'm not sure it reaches my eyes. I need to get this over with. "Can we talk for a second?"

The line between his eyebrows deepens. "Sure, what's up?"

"Well, first… I owe you an apology. I'm sorry I threw myself at you last night."

Chase looks over my head, presumably to make sure no one is around, then takes me by the upper arm and leads me to another hallway, a little more out of the main area. He looks down at me with drawn brows. "You have nothing to apologize for."

"I do. You clearly weren't interested, and I kept pushing it." My cheeks heat in embarrassment at the foggy memory of me undressing unprovoked once we were in his bedroom.

"Twyla, I was very interested. Don't mistake my wanting to show you respect and make sure you were making the best decision for yourself for disinterest. Do you know how hard it was to keep my mind on the game today and not fixate on how you looked in that bra and underwear set last night?" He pushes a hand through his damp hair.

"Really?" Some of the tension in my neck eases.

"Really. But it was an emotional day for you, and you'd had a lot to drink. If you decide you want to do that with me, I want to know you're not going to regret it."

"I do want to do that. I won't regret it," I say boldly and step closer to him.

His nostrils flare and his eyelids dip down. I'd love to know what he's thinking right now, but he simply nods. "What was the other thing?"

"Huh?"

"You started with first, implying there was a second."

"Oh, right." I emerge from my stupor. "I'm sorry you had to get in a fight last night because of me."

His eyebrows draw down. "Make no mistake about it, that was all them, not you. They were disrespectful and should've backed off when you told them to."

I nod in agreement. "I guess I'm not *that* sorry because I still think it was superhot watching you defend my honor."

He laughs and shakes his head.

"I blame the muscles."

Before he responds, I hear my brother's voice behind him. "There you guys are."

We both stiffen and Chase's eyes widen, looking at me in surprise and concern. He turns and steps aside so I can see Miles, showered and changed.

"What are you guys doing?" He looks between us with a small frown.

"Chase found me wandering and was going to show me the way to the locker room. It doesn't matter how many times I'm here; this place is like a maze." I walk past Chase to my brother and give him a hug. "Great game."

"Thanks, sis."

"Is Heather here?" I ask, changing the subject.

"No, she couldn't make it." I don't sense much disappointment on his end.

"That's too bad. I'm assuming we're going for dinner since you guys won?"

Miles looks over me at Chase. "Yeah, you coming, man?"

I force myself not to turn and look at Chase, but I wait for his answer with bated breath. It would be easier to pretend if he weren't there, but I want to spend all the time I can with him.

"Yeah, I'll be there," he says.

"Great. Sis, you can ride with me. Just let me grab my bag from the locker room."

I nod.

"I gotta get my stuff too," Chase says.

Miles is already off, heading back toward the locker room, and Chase's and my eyes catch as he passes me. There's no mistaking the guilt in his expression that I'm sure matches my own.

twenty

. . .

Chase

Dinner is a long, torturous affair because I end up at the opposite end of the table from Twyla, stuck across from Violet and Brady, who just want to talk wedding plans and kiss.

I'm happy for them both, but I don't give two shits whether her dress is white, off-white, ivory, or blush. I mean, isn't it all basically the same anyway?

Maybe it's better that I'm not close to Twyla when Miles is around anyway. I felt like the biggest douchebag back at the arena when he stumbled upon us. Things would be a hell of a lot easier if I wasn't attracted to his little sister, but as it is, the woman has a choke hold on me. The number of times I've glanced down the table at Twyla and imagined throwing her over my shoulder again, finding some closet, and rutting into her like a bull isn't great.

I cut into my steak when Brady leans over and speaks in a low voice, "So what's the deal with you two?"

I manage to keep my composure, bringing the piece of meat to my mouth and not even glancing at him. "What are you talking about?"

"C'mon, man. You've looked down the table a hundred

times tonight. I know what it's like when you're into someone so bad you can't take your eyes off them. Does she know you're into her?"

I turn my head, glancing across the table to make sure Violet isn't listening. She's talking to Bryce about something that happened at Theo's school this week.

"And if she did?" I arch an eyebrow.

Brady raises both hands. "I wouldn't say a word. As far as I'm concerned, you're consenting adults. That said, it would probably go over better with Miles if you told him before anything happened between you guys."

I stare at him for a beat, then glance down the table at Twyla, who catches my eye before I look back at Brady. "It hasn't gotten that far."

He claps me on the shoulder. "Well, just don't hurt her. I think that's ultimately what would send Miles over the edge."

"Believe me, I have no intention of doing that."

He nods and releases my shoulder.

For the rest of the meal, I do my best to not glance in Twyla's direction. Clearly I'm more obvious than I thought if Brady's noticed my interest.

That becomes impossible at the end of dinner when Twyla calls down the table, "Chase, would you mind if I caught a ride home with you to save Miles the trip?"

Everyone's head turns toward me, and I do my best to project a calm, unruffled effect. "Yeah, no problem."

"Thanks, man," Miles says.

Once again, I feel like an ass. He thinks I'm doing it out of the goodness of my heart when really I'm going to be pawing at his sister the minute I'm alone with her.

With my lips pressed together, I nod.

We all finish up and stand in front of the restaurant, saying our goodbyes. Brady gives me a look I can't interpret before he and Violet head off toward their vehicle.

"Thanks for the hookup to the game today," Twyla says to Miles and gives him a hug.

"Always." He pulls away but continues to hold her by the shoulders. "You really are okay? I know yesterday had to be tough."

"I'm fine. Stop worrying about me." She rolls her eyes.

"It's my job as your big brother," he says.

"Well, take a day off once in a while, would you?" She chuckles.

Miles lets his hands drop, then looks at me. "Thanks for letting my sister ride with you. Drive safe, yeah?"

"Oh my god, stop!" Twyla throws her hands up in exasperation. "Chase can get me home safely." She shakes her head at her brother, who grins at me.

He obviously added that last bit just to annoy her.

"All right, let's get going before you want to punch him," I say.

"Seriously." She shakes her head as she walks beside me to my truck.

Miles heads the other way in the parking lot.

Though the urge to touch her, even just hold her hand, is strong once we're both in my truck, I refrain. There's still a chance someone from the team could see us. Instead, I start the truck and drive to our condo building. The drive takes about twenty minutes with traffic, and we don't talk about much of any consequence on the way.

The tension in the cab is thick and feels as if it increases with every yard we draw closer to our building. I wonder if she's like me and thinking about what might happen when we get inside one of our places. The cab is filled with the cucumber scent of her shampoo, and I'm aware of every small movement she makes in the seat next to me.

As we approach the condo, I click the button on my visor to open the garage door to the underground parking, then drive down the ramp and into my designated parking spot.

I turn off the engine and turn to look at Twyla. "Here we are."

"Here we are," she mimics, and our gazes lock and hold.

And then we're both diving forward to meet the other in the middle. I grip the back of her head as my tongue plunges into her mouth. She meets me stroke for stroke, and a frisson of electricity heads straight to my dick that's straining the confines of my suit pants.

Then I'm gripping her by the waist and pulling her on top of me. Her hands land on either side of my face and she leans in to continue our kiss. I palm the back of her head and push my hips up into her. She moans into my mouth and bears down on me, rolling her hips in search of the friction she needs.

The sound of someone's car beeping after the owner has locked their door has her stripping her lips from me. "We should take this inside before someone sees us."

She's right, I know she is, but I groan my dissent anyway before picking her up by the waist and depositing her back in the passenger seat. I waste no time getting out of the truck and walking around to open the passenger side door for her. Twyla smiles and I help her out of the truck, keeping her hand in mine as we make our way to the elevator.

I so badly want to push her into a corner of the elevator car and place my lips on hers again, but I know from experience that the elevator will stop in the lobby to pick up some more passengers and they'd get an eyeful if I try to sneak even one kiss. I doubt I can refrain from devouring her.

Three people hop on when the elevator stops at the lobby, and the ascent takes forever. Finally, the elevator reaches the thirty-third floor and the doors slide open. Twyla and I walk fast down the hallway, her hand in mine.

"Your place or mine?" I ask when we're close to our apartments.

"Yours," she says in a breathy voice that I hope is from

being turned on and not because we're almost running down the hall.

I miss the key in the lock twice because of shaking hands from needing this woman so badly. When I finally manage to get the key in the hole, I push open the door. Twyla walks right past me, paying no mind to Zeus, who is meowing for her attention, and heads straight to the hallway. I lock the door then follow her to my bedroom, closing the door on Zeus when he attempts to follow.

I turn to face her, where she's standing in the middle of the room, chest heaving with breath.

"Last chance to opt out," I say.

"Not a chance."

We take a few steps toward one another and collide in the middle. Our mouths meet and my hands roam down to her ass, pulling her up so her legs are around my waist. She's so much smaller than me that it barely takes any effort to keep her there, and I decide then and there that I'll be fucking her like this at some point.

Twyla's tits rub against my chest as I deepen the kiss, moving it from uncontrolled lust to something slightly more patient. I want to bask in the slow slide of our tongues as I deepen the kiss and inhale her scent, committing this to memory.

I walk us over to the bed. When the mattress hits my calves, I bend and lay Twyla down. She stares up at me, lids half-drawn, as I straighten up. I crouch to take her left leg and remove her shoe, then the other one. She sits up and watches me silently as I undress her. I pull her shirt up over her head, revealing her navy lace bra.

Unable to help myself, I run my tongue along the swell of her breast up to her collarbone, which I suck gently for a moment. Twyla sighs and her hand goes to the back of my head. I repeat the same motion on the other side and dip down farther to pull her stiff nipple into my mouth through the thin fabric, pressing her back against the mattress.

Her back arches. "That feels so good, Chase."

All I want to do is to make her feel good, so I do it again until I become too impatient and undo her pants before sliding them down her legs.

This is it. I'm going to see Twyla naked for the first time. The woman I've been fantasizing about and masturbating to for years.

I press the clip that rests between her breasts and they spring free, the scraps of lace still clinging to her nipples until I slowly drag them off. Twyla takes a quick breath.

Next, I slide her underwear down her legs, tossing it behind me. Then I straighten up and take a moment to just take her in. Naked in my bed, ready and wanton and more beautiful than any woman I've ever seen. Her riot of curls lie scattered around her head on the mattress and I know without a doubt that my favorite hairstyle of hers will be when it has that just-fucked look.

"Your turn."

I expect her to be somewhat shy our first time together, but this woman is looking at me as if she wants to eat me up. It makes my already hard cock push with even greater force against the fabric of my pants.

Twyla sits up then stands and takes a few steps so she's in front of me. I can't help myself—I palm her breasts, rubbing my thumbs over her nipples.

Her eyes flutter closed. "Now you're distracting me from getting you undressed."

"Do you want me to stop?"

She shakes her head. "No, but I want you naked too, so you probably should."

After tweaking her nipples between my thumbs and fore-fingers, I drop my hands and help her push off my suit jacket, then watch as she loosens my tie. I yank it off while she undoes my dress shirt button by button, and I pull it out from being tucked into my pants. My heart pounds with anticipation by the time her hands slide up and over my chest to push the fabric over my shoulders, allowing it to fall to the floor.

She undoes my belt. As I watch, I can barely believe we're here, about to do this. I've thought of Twyla so much over the years, but she was with that asshat, so I never actually entertained the idea that this day would come.

She slides my belt out of the loops, tosses it to the floor, then undoes the button and zipper on my dress pants. I help her push the waistband of my boxer briefs past my engorged cock, then I step out of my pants so that we both stand naked in front of each other.

"Wow," she says with what sounds like awe.

"What?"

"I know I saw you in the shower the one time, but this is the first time I've really gotten to see you like this. You basically have the perfect body." Her fingers run over my chest and down across my abs.

"I think you have the two of us confused, sunshine." I pick her up and deposit her in the middle of the bed. "Here, let me show you."

twenty-one

. . .

Twyla

C hase sets me gently in the middle of the bed and I stare up at him in awe.

His body is perfection. I don't even think he realizes how sexy he is, which only adds to the appeal. I have to press my thighs together to stem some of the need pulsing between my legs.

But he's not down with that. He shakes his head, puts a hand on each knee, and spreads my legs, wedging himself between my thighs, which isn't an easy feat given the breadth of his muscled shoulders.

I don't know what it is with him, but I feel as though I can be free with him sexually. Maybe it's the fact that I caught him masturbating to thoughts of me already and I boldly followed suit, or maybe it's just how comfortable and safe he makes me feel whenever I'm around him. I'm not self-conscious. I don't feel the need to cover up or present my best angle, suck in my stomach, or wonder what I look like *down there*.

He obviously likes what he sees because he licks his lips and looks up at me, meeting my gaze as he spreads me with his thumbs and swipes my clit with his tongue. I moan and twist my hips, but his big hands clamp down on my legs, holding me in place.

His tongue flicks at my clit until I'm a panting mess, then he turns his attention to my entrance. The sensation is no less intense as he fucks me with his tongue.

My hands roam my body, squeezing my breasts while I moan. "Chase, that's so good."

"That's it, tell me what you like," he murmurs against my sensitive flesh.

He swipes me a few times from ass to clit and I can't hold back the sounds desperate to escape. When he suckles my clit, I arch my hips up off the bed, but he follows me up, eyes locked with mine and unwavering while his mouth continues its magic.

"Oh god, I'm close. I'm sooo close," I shout.

The sensation intensifies and concentrates in my core until it's too much to contain and I come apart, writhing, body strung as tight as a bow until I fall lax against the mattress.

Chase gently laps up my release then looks at me from between my legs. "Fuck, you even taste like sunshine."

I don't know what that means, but as I lie in the aftermath of my orgasm, I know it's good because he's licking his lips as though he's just had the best meal ever.

"That was… wow," I say, finally finding words.

"That was just the beginning."

"Promise?" I say in a breathy voice that makes him chuckle.

"Promise." He kisses the inside of my thigh and comes to lie next to me, head propped up on his hand.

His fingers trace over my body—lightly, rhythmically, and with just enough pressure to leave me wanting more. Chase brings his lips to mine and I don't hesitate to move my hands into his hair and deepen the kiss. While we kiss, his hand finds its way between my thighs, lightly coasting over my clit.

I pull back from our kiss. "Again?" I ask, eyebrows raised.

"Gotta get you ready for me, sunshine." He pushes two large fingers into me and curves them.

I swear my eyes roll back into my head.

"I don't want to hurt you." He leans down and draws a nipple into his mouth, swirling his tongue around the turgid tip.

This feels a lot like being worshipped and it's not something I'm used to. With Mathew, I was the one doing most of the work during foreplay. I'm not used to lying back and letting a man devour me. But I love it.

Chase fucks me with his fingers, and I can't stop myself from pumping my hips to the cadence he's set as another orgasm builds. When he adds a third finger, there's a bite of pain, but he curves them and brushes against my G-spot. The feeling is intense and makes me feel out of control which would normally bother me, but I know I'm in good hands with Chase.

"You okay?" he asks before moving to my other breast and nipping at my nipple.

"Yeah."

He moves his fingers in a way that he's not really pulling them in and out of me, but it lights the fuse on the firecracker that is my climax. The constant attention on my G-spot has me coming as he sucks one nipple hard and I convulse under him.

My head rocks back and forth in the aftermath, unable to believe that I've had two of the most powerful orgasms of my life back to back with this man.

Chase rolls away from me and gets up off the bed. I'm too sated to turn my head and see what he's doing, but soon he's standing at the edge of the bed with a condom on, stroking himself.

It's a good thing he prepared me because he is big. Certainly bigger than any man I've ever been with. I shouldn't be surprised—everything about Chase is big.

"Can't wait to be between those thighs, sunshine."

His term of endearment makes me smile and I reach my arms out for him. He crawls the short distance to me.

"How do you want it?" I ask, wanting to please him as much as he's pleased me.

His brown eyes flare open for a moment. "I want you to ride me."

I sit up and grin. "My pleasure." Literally.

He lays his big body down in the middle of the bed and I crawl over him from his feet up, sticking out my tongue and licking up his hard length.

"Jesus. As much as I want that right now, I want to be inside you a helluva lot more."

"I aim to please." I straddle his waist and reach back to grip his cock, then I rise up over it, positioning the wide head at my entrance. I sink down as far as I can, my eyes fluttering closed. I rise up and sink down a few more inches, repeating the process a few times before he's fully seated inside me.

"You good?" Chase asks. The concern in his voice only endears him to me more.

I open my eyes and smirk. "So good."

He relaxes and I move over him. Chase watches with rapture as I work myself into a frenzy, then his huge hands cup my breasts. The feeling of him holding me makes me roll my hips, applying just the right amount of pressure on my clit. Sweat beads on my skin as I work myself closer to my orgasm. I'm a panting, writhing mess.

"That's it. You look so fucking hot right now. Do you know how many times I've thought about your pussy squeezing my cock like this?"

Chase's words catapult me past the finish line, and I feel myself clench around his length. We both groan as I ride out the waves of pleasure until I eventually flop down onto his hard chest to catch my breath.

His hands weave through the tangled, curly mess that is my hair, and he kisses the top of my head. "Damn, sunshine."

He's still hard inside me and I shimmy my hips, needing him to move even though I just came. Chase chuckles in my ear and sits up, kissing me deeply before pulling me off him and setting me aside.

God, it's so hot how his physical strength allows him to manhandle me. I love it.

I'm sitting on the bed, waiting for him to make his move. It doesn't take long. He positions himself behind me, and without him having to say a word, I get on my hands and knees, back arched and ass up.

He spreads my ass cheeks with his hands and licks through my center, causing a full-body shiver. "Couldn't resist," he says in a gravelly voice.

I merely hum my approval. With one hand on my waist, he lines up his cock with my entrance and pushes slowly inside. We moan in unison.

He's so deep inside me like this. I've never felt this full and I'm desperate for him to move, but he holds himself there for a moment, giving me time to adjust. While he waits, he squeezes my ass then rubs his hand over it in a soothing gesture.

When he pulls out and pushes himself back in, it's as if every pleasure point in my body is focused on my core. I push back against him, wanting more, needing him to know he doesn't have to be gentle. He takes the hint and thrusts into me with more force.

Within a minute he's like a pile driver, drilling into me so hard my teeth shake, but God, do I love it. The sounds he's making, the way his fingertips press into the flesh at my hips, and all the cursing that leaves his mouth like he can barely handle what's going on.

We find the perfect rhythm and I push back into him so that the only sound in the room is our heavy breathing and the slapping sound of when we come together. Chase's hand drifts around my waist and settles on my clit, gently rubbing.

I shake my head. "No, I can't come again."

"Yes, you can." The determination in his voice suggests that he won't let himself come until I do.

The need to come builds inside me again, but this time it fills me with a desperation I don't think I've ever felt before. It builds and builds and builds, and when he pinches my clit, I go off like a firework exploding colors in the sky. Chase groans low in his chest, jerks into me a few more times, and holds himself there, emptying himself into the condom.

I drop forward onto the bed, completely spent. Chase falls beside me, resting his hand on my lower back as though he wants to maintain contact with me.

"I've never come that many times in one night," I murmur into the comforter.

"The night is still young. We're just getting started." He rolls to his side so he's looking at me.

I turn my head and open my eyes to look at him. "You're trying to kill me." I chuckle.

"What a way to go though, right?"

"The best." My eyes drift closed of their own accord.

Chase picks me up and positions me with my head near the pillows. He pulls the blanket over me then walks around the bed and gets in on the other side, moving over enough so that he's spooning me from behind.

He kisses the back of my head. "You go to sleep now. There will be plenty of time for more orgasms later."

I mumble something in response, though I'm not sure what. I drift off into a contented sleep with professional football's biggest, grumpiest player wrapped around me. Pure bliss.

Who would have thought that Chase Andrews was a cuddler?

———

I wake to a warm body pressed against my back, and this time I know it's not Zeus because of the large arm draped over my waist. That, and the erection poking into my ass.

Smiling into my pillow, I relive last night in my head—the killer orgasms, how strong Chase is but how gentle he is at the same time, the way his eyes devoured me... and his mouth. I moan into my pillow, wanting more. No man has ever made me feel the way Chase has—in and out of the bedroom.

"If you keep making those noises, I'm not responsible for my actions." Chase's rough morning voice sounds from behind me, and I giggle.

"Is that right?" I wiggle my ass and his arm clamps down on my hip.

"Careful, sunshine. I'm getting ideas."

"Good."

Chase squeezes me into him tighter.

My gaze snags on the nightstand and I spot the book I dropped off for him to read for our little "book club," the bookmark stuck nearly midway through the book.

"Shoot. Did I sleep on your side last night? All your stuff is over here." I roll onto my back so I can see him.

He props himself up on his elbow and looks down at me. "I don't care what side of my bed you sleep on, just as long as you're in it."

Stretching, I smile and pick up the copy of Everly Ashton's *Hit or Miss* and open the book to see what part he's at. "I can't believe you're actually reading this." I look down at him.

"I said I would," he says matter-of-factly.

"I know, but I wasn't sure you really would once you started. A lot of guys think romance books are just for women."

"They don't know what they're missing. I'm getting all kinds of good tips in that thing." He chuckles.

I can't control my grin. "Oh yeah, like what?"

Chase casts kisses on my neck. "Like the fact that women think and talk about sex almost as much as men."

"Mmm, okay, what else?" I ask in a breathy voice.

He makes his way up to my earlobe and pinches it between his teeth. "And I know that women want to be wooed by the man pursuing them."

"Well, I await my wooing."

He pulls the sheet down from over my breasts and leans in to suckle my nipple. I toss the book to the floor and bring my hand up to his head.

"I consider what we did last night part of wooing. How'd I do?" Chase bites my nipple then soothes the pain with a few swipes of his tongue.

"A plus, but I think I might need a refresher this morning."

Chase makes his way down my body, dragging his tongue to the edge of the sheet before he pushes the sheet all the way off. He climbs over me, using his shoulders to spread my thighs, situating himself between them. "I pride myself in always putting my full effort into anything I do. Let's see if I can make more of a lasting impression this time."

He parts me and swipes his tongue from top to bottom while I moan. And he's right—the impression he makes isn't one that will leave me for a long, long time.

twenty-two

· · ·

Chase

Tuesday is another rest day for me, and knowing we can't spend another full day in bed together, I suggest to Twyla that we head over the bridge to Muir Woods. I mean, I could easily spend another day in bed with Twyla, but I don't want her thinking my only interest in her is her pussy.

The woods aren't far, and I like to go there when the pace of the city feels like too much. Spending time in nature is always soul soothing, and sharing it with Twyla will make it that much better.

I lend Twyla one of my extra backpacks, and we pack water and snacks and head out. It's pretty busy at the trailhead, but once we've been walking for half an hour, the crowds thin out until we can't see anyone ahead or behind us on the trail. Perfect. The massive redwoods soar high over us, and the scent of the forest relaxes me as always.

"What are you up to for the rest of the week?" I ask.

"I volunteer at the school for the first time tomorrow, so I'm looking forward to that. It's not the same as teaching, but it will be a nice way to spend some of my time while I'm here."

The mention that she's not here permanently is a good reminder for me not to get too invested in whatever this is. I'm probably a rebound for Twyla, seeing as she recently got out of an engagement, and I need to remember she has a life on the other side of the country.

"I'm sure all the kids will love you."

"Here's hoping. I don't usually have any problems with that, but sometimes some kids hold out and have a chip on their shoulder for one reason or another. It just makes me work that much harder to figure out what's going on with them and how I can help."

I smile at the dirt ground. I've never seen Twyla with her students, but I can imagine that she's an amazing teacher. She'll make an amazing mother one day.

I stop walking for a second at that thought. Why the hell am I thinking about what kind of mother Twyla will be?

"You okay?" she asks, and I look into her doe eyes peering at me.

"Yeah." I clear my throat. "They're lucky to have you. I've been meaning to bring up the subject of your brother."

Twyla's steps slow. "What about him?"

I stop and turn to face her. "Do you think we should tell him what's going on with us? It already felt like a betrayal before we slept together. Now…"

She thinks about it for a moment and shakes her head. "It's none of his business. I'm an adult. Besides…"

She doesn't need to finish her sentence for me to know what she was going to say. We don't even know what this is or how long it will last. Likely, just the duration of her time in California. Then she'll go home with a clear head, having had some rebound sex and put her ex behind her, ready to pick up her life where she left it—minus the broken heart.

I pull the baseball cap off my head, fix my hair, and put it back on. "Okay, it's your call."

"I don't want to tell him." Her voice is firm.

Piper Rayne

I nod. I don't feel good about her decision, but I'll respect it just the same.

We come to where the trail veers off in several directions. We look at the map to choose one that isn't too long or changes elevations too much—since today is a rest day for me —and head on our way.

We've been on the trail for about half an hour when Twyla's phone rings inside her bag.

"I'm surprised you even got a signal here," I say while she takes off the backpack and locates her phone.

When she pulls it out, her face goes blank. "It's Mathew," she says in a monotone voice then looks at me. "I don't know what to do. I saw that he called yesterday too, but I missed the call because…"

She doesn't have to finish her sentence. I know exactly why she missed the call. Because we spent the whole day together in bed, trading orgasms.

Irritation flares in my chest, but I keep it at bay.

"Do you want him calling you?" Regardless of my jealousy, I'm not the boss of Twyla. She can do what she wants. But if this loser is bugging her when she doesn't want to be bothered, that's a different story.

She shakes her head. "No. I told him last time to leave me alone."

Decision made.

I hold out my hand. "Accept the call and give me your phone."

Her bottom lip trembles, but she does what I ask, placing the phone face up in my palm.

I bring it to my ear and hear a guy say, "Finally. Twyla, I—"

"Hey, Mathew?" I don't bother waiting for him to reply. "Twyla made it clear the last time you guys spoke that she doesn't want you bothering her, so if you know what's good for you, you'll stop harassing her and lose this number."

"Who is this?" he says.

"Someone who will do what it takes to make sure her loser ex, who's probably just now figuring out what he lost, doesn't make it any harder for her to move on with her life. That's a promise. Don't make me make good on that promise, Mathew. You won't like it."

I click End on the call and hold the phone back out to Twyla, who's staring at me with a strange expression I can't decipher. Hopefully she's not pissed at me. She had to know when she handed me the phone that I wasn't going to have a heart-to-heart with the guy.

"Thank you," she says in a soft voice and slides the phone out of my hand.

"You're welcome. Make sure you let me know if he gives you any more trouble."

She nods and slides the phone into her backpack.

When we walk again, Twyla is noticeably quieter than she was before Mathew's call. Jesus, is she thinking about that asshole? But a few minutes later, I second-guess that being the reason for her quiet contemplation when we come across a particularly big tree. It has to be at least ten or twelve feet wide.

There are no rails on the side of the dirt path here, so Twyla steps off to examine the tree closer. "It's insane to me how big these trees are." She walks the circumference of the tree until she ends up on the side that faces away from the path.

I follow her. "I know. Think of how many hundreds and thousands of years some of these have been here."

When I reach her, she turns to face me. "You know, I've always wanted to fool around outdoors."

Her words are like a shot of adrenaline to my dick. "Is that right?"

"Mmmhmm." She nods and walks to me before rising up on her tiptoes.

I bend and kiss her, pulling her in closer. Her hand slides between us and squeezes my cock that's rapidly growing in size.

"What did you have in mind?" I ask, glancing up and around to make sure no one is around.

Even if they were, you can't see the trail from where we are on the other side of this big tree. The forest is quiet, with only the rustle of a faint breeze and the occasional sound of a bird or a twig snapping as something makes its way across the forest floor.

Without answering, Twyla drops to her knees, leaving no doubt as to what she has in mind. I let my backpack slide down my arms and deposit it on the forest floor. She licks her lips as she pulls down the waistband of my sports shorts until they slide down to my ankles. I pull my T-shirt up and hold it under my chin because I want to see every second of this. Twyla's hand drifts up over the ridges of my lower abdomen before going back down to palm my erection through the cotton of my boxer briefs. I groan while my hips jerk forward of their own accord. Then finally she pulls the briefs down and my cock springs free.

Fuck, how many times have I imagined this exact scenario? Somehow, the reality of having Twyla on her knees in front of me is a thousand times better than all my dirtiest fantasies combined.

The moment she trails her tongue from the bottom to the top of my cock, then grips the base, she has my full attention. The forest could be burning down around us and I wouldn't be able to look away.

This is the first time she's given me head. I've been too focused on giving her as many orgasms as possible and not on myself. But I am not complaining now. I'm happy to take what she wants to give.

She sucks the head of my cock between her lips. I swear I've never seen anything hotter in my life. Her eyes flick up to watch my reaction and I imagine that what she sees is a man in awe of what's going on in front of him.

When she pumps me with the hand at my base and sucks on the head again, a small groan leaves my lips. She repeats the motion several times and I bring my hand to the back of her head, gripping her ponytail.

Twyla's mouth slides down my cock, her lips stretched wide as she takes as much as she can of me. Fuck, the visual of this alone is almost enough to make me come, never mind the sensation of her lips. She bobs up and down on my cock until her saliva covers it and drips down her chin.

When I grip her ponytail tighter, it only spurs her on. At one point she pushes me in until I breach the back of her throat and she holds herself there, staring up at me with her big, bright eyes.

"Goddamn, woman." My voice is as rough as the bark on the tree behind her.

She removes her hand from my base, and I thrust into her mouth, hand still on her ponytail. Twyla opens wide, letting me set the pace while I fuck her mouth. The base of my spine tingles and I pick up my pace, gripping her hair tightly while I push my length in and out past her plump lips.

That's when the sound of someone coming down the trail reaches us—voices reverberating through the forest. My eyes flick down to meet hers as I still. But Twyla's not having it. She moves up and down my cock, picking up the rhythm I was just working.

My balls tighten and the base of my spine tingles even more. I hunch over her, one hand in her hair, the other pressed into the bark of the tree behind her as I come down her throat, mouth open on a silent moan as the people pass the tree we're behind, none the wiser.

It takes me a moment to feel sturdy enough on my feet to straighten and remove my hand from the tree. When I do, my chest heaves as though I just ran a hundred yards.

I hold my hand out to help Twyla up first, then I pull my boxer briefs and shorts back up.

"That rocked my world." I pull Twyla into me, kissing the top of her head before bending to really kiss her. I taste myself on her tongue, but it doesn't bother me.

This experience is something I'll never forget. In fact, I'll probably have a hard-on every time I walk in Muir Woods now.

"You've been so generous. I had to return the favor." She rests her chin on my chest and stares up at me. "And like I said, I've always wanted to do it outside. The fear of being caught is kind of a turn-on."

I chuckle. "We almost did get caught."

She puts her finger in the air. "Almost. But we didn't."

I kiss her forehead. "I wouldn't have cared anyway."

She smacks me in the chest. "You would have cared if it was all over the media."

"Nope. Still worth it."

Twyla laughs, which I'm starting to realize is one of my favorite sounds in the world, and we get ourselves organized again and continue down the trail.

I don't generally like surprises of any kind, but it turns out that Twyla showing up in town was the best kind of surprise there is.

twenty-three

. . .

Twyla

"There's no trading lunches, guys." I walk over to the four desks that are pushed together into a group and take the rice crispy square from the little boy and hand it back to the little blonde girl who gave it to him.

"But they're his favorite," she says with a pout.

I crouch beside her desk. "Mine too. But do you know why we're not allowed to trade anything in our lunches with anyone else?"

She shakes her head.

"Because some people have really bad allergies, and if they eat something they're not supposed to, they can get really sick. You don't want your friend here to get sick, do you?" I motion to the boy across from her.

She shakes her head. "No. And Bryon is my boyfriend, not my friend."

The other two kids in the group of four giggle.

"Well then, you especially wouldn't want to get your boyfriend sick."

"I don't want Byron to be sick!" Her brown eyes grow wide.

"Okay then, from now on, everyone should just eat whatever their parents packed them for lunch, okay?"

She nods. "Okay, Miss Cavanaugh."

"Thank you." I stand again and check on the rest of the kids.

Once the kids are finished with their allotted eating time, we all head outside so they can burn off some of their energy before class starts back up. I can leave after lunch, but I offer to stay and supervise outdoors since Violet is also one of the monitors, figuring we can chat and catch up while watching the kids.

She finds me a few minutes after we arrive outside.

"Hey, how did it go?" she asks.

"It was good. Everyone behaved."

"I'm sure this is easy for you, you're used to it, but I was petrified the first day when the teacher left me with that many kids. A few I can handle, but twenty plus…" Her eyes widen.

I laugh. "I'm sure you did fine. Where is Theo?"

Violet points toward the basketball court where he's trying to dribble the ball with a few of his friends.

"He must like having you in the classroom, I bet."

She nods. "Yeah, he does. Hannah helps out on school trips when she can, but she can never commit to helping all the time because of her work schedule. I think he likes knowing someone will be here every day with him."

"Makes sense. How are things with Hannah now that you and Brady are engaged?"

Hannah is Theo's mom and Brady's ex. They tried to make it work after she got pregnant after a one-night stand, but from what I understand, they figured out quickly that they were better off as friends.

"She's been great. Nothing but supportive, and I think she understands I'm not trying to replace her or anything, but that I want Theo to know I'm here for him if he needs me."

I bump her with my shoulder. "You're a lucky woman."

"I am." She fingers the large engagement ring on her left hand. "Speaking of lucky... have you gotten lucky since I last saw you?"

My cheeks heat. "Why do you ask?"

She leans back a bit and eyes me up and down. "You seem more... relaxed, maybe more... satisfied?"

I bring my hands to my face. "God, am I that obvious?"

She chuckles. "Not to everyone. Is it Chase?" Violet waits with bated breath.

I nod.

"Ah!" she cries out, causing a few of the kids to look in our direction. "I knew you guys were into each other."

I whip my head around and look at her. "How did you know?"

"Well first, he willingly showed up at your house of his own accord. And second, he may have admitted to Brady that he had a thing for you."

I hate the warm, squishy feeling in my belly like we're thirteen and these are our first crushes. It feels a lot like hope, but I have to remember that Chase and I haven't even had a conversation about what our sleeping together means long term. I don't have any idea if he wants a girlfriend or how that could even work with my home being on the other side of the country. Not to mention the hurdle that is my brother.

"What did he say exactly?" I'm digging, but I can't help it. I want to hear what Chase said about me.

"I didn't get any specifics from Brady, but I guess he caught Chase looking at you a bunch of times at the team dinner after the game and called him out on it. He didn't deny it."

I'm surprised, honestly. Chase is such a private person that I figured he would have just denied it. Suddenly, it dawns on me that if Brady noticed...

"And my brother?"

Violet waves off my concern. "Brady wouldn't say anything, and as far as I know, Miles hasn't said that he suspects something."

I release a relieved breath. "Good."

Violet cocks her head to the side. "But… won't you have to tell Miles eventually?"

My shoulders slump. "Maybe. Maybe not. I don't even know exactly what's going on between us. We haven't discussed what any of it means."

"I guess the question is, do you *want* it to mean something?"

"That's the million-dollar question, isn't it?"

But it's one I can't answer yet.

———

That evening, I walk into Chase's condo and find him lying on the couch with Zeus asleep on his big chest and I'm pretty sure my ovaries combust.

"Should I be jealous?" I joke.

He shakes his head. "Nah, I'd take your pussy over this one any day."

His words make me blush, but I secretly thrill.

"Noted." He taps the spot next to him on the couch, so I sit down, book in hand. "Are you ready for our first official book club meeting?"

"I have no idea." When I give him a quizzical look, he explains. "I read the book. Beyond that, I'm not sure what to expect."

"We'll just chat about it. I prepared some questions to generate conversation and we can share our favorite quotes, favorite parts of the book. Anything goes really."

"I'll do my best, but I can't promise I'll have comments as insightful as your book club in Connecticut."

I give him a chaste kiss on the lips. "Thank you for doing

this for me. Now where's your book? You might need to reference it."

"It's on the dresser in my bedroom. Can you get it?" He gives me the cutest little pleading look and I picture him trying to use this on his parents when he was little. "I don't want to have to wake Zeus."

I can't help but chuckle. "For a guy who seemed to not be into the cat at all at first, you sure seem to like him now."

"He's growing on me," he reluctantly admits.

With another laugh, I get off the couch and retrieve the book, passing it to him and picking up mine from where I left it on the couch cushion. I made annotations in my book and added tabs where there's something I want to discuss.

"Wow, you even color-coordinated all your little tabs."

I look at the book with pride. The cover is mostly hot pink with light blue and white and I've used the same colors for my tabs.

"It's a bookish thing," I say, and he gives me an indulgent smile. I open the book to the first marker. "All right, the first thing I wanted to chat about was some of the obstacles the hero and heroine felt stood in their way when they first met… besides the fact that she accidentally shot him."

"I liked that part," he says.

"That's such a guy thing to say." I playfully roll my eyes and shake my head. "So, Ollie felt like the ten-year age gap was an issue, while Jemma initially was concerned about the perceived status difference since he's a children's heart surgeon and she's an elementary teacher. Do you think either of those things should be an issue for them?"

"I don't think any of that shit makes a difference. What matters is how they feel about each other and how they treat each other. End of."

I contemplate his answer and decide to play devil's advocate. "True, but don't you think societal pressures can play into the dynamic of a relationship? For instance, if everyone around them had an issue with one or both of those things, don't you think it would weigh on them and eventually creep into their dynamic with each other?"

Chase studies me for a beat. "Are you asking because you're a teacher and I'm a professional athlete?"

I blink in shock. The thought honestly hadn't occurred to me. "No, not at all. I'm just talking about the book."

"Okay, because if you are—"

"Honestly, Chase. I'm just talking about the book and relationships in general. Besides, it's not like we're in an official relationship, right?"

I couldn't help myself, I had to say the words. We haven't talked about what, if anything, this all means. The opportunity to fish for information presented itself and I couldn't let it pass by.

"Right, of course. Yeah," he says in a gruff voice.

I hate the disappointment that comes over me. Hate myself for getting my hopes up when I knew I shouldn't. I didn't really think we were in a relationship, but I guess I was hoping he'd answer differently. The messed-up part is that I don't even know what I wish he'd said. Just that it wasn't that.

"Okay, then the question stands. Don't you think the outside pressure would affect their relationship?"

We chat for another twenty minutes about the book before Chase says, "Hey, I have an idea."

"What's that?"

"Why don't we act out some of our favorite scenes in the book?"

I grin. "I know your favorite scenes."

"I liked that one where they had sex in front of the mirror."

"Oh you did, did you?" I arch an eyebrow.

"Mmmhmm. I was thinking of that big mirror that runs across the vanity in my en suite."

I lean so I'm bending over him, our mouths only a few inches apart. "You'd have to move Zeus off your chest and wake him."

"It's a sacrifice I'm willing to make." Without hesitation, he lifts Zeus from his chest and sits up, setting him on the floor.

Zeus stretches his front legs and yawns, looking up at us with a sleepy, pissed-off expression.

Chase stands and looks down at him. "Sorry, buddy, we have to go finish our book club meeting." Then he bends and lifts me up over his shoulder.

I yelp and pretend I don't love it, although I do. When we reach the en suite, we reenact the scene from the book, only better.

When we're finished, Chase looks at me in the mirror and says while panting, "I love book club."

"Best book club ever."

We seal our declaration with a kiss.

twenty-four

. . .

Chase

"I still don't understand what I'm doing wrong." Twyla stomps her foot on the scuffed wood floor like a child and I have to hold back a laugh because I don't think she'll appreciate it.

She's cute as fuck when she's frustrated, and this is the first time I've seen her like this. It's kind of turning me on, but everything she does lately turns me on.

We're at The Crooked Nail, where I challenged her to a game of darts.

I step up behind her. "Try not to lean forward when you throw and keep your dart hand closer to your body." I reach around and grab her wrist, drawing it in a little closer to her head. "Like this."

The press of her back to my front and the scent of her cucumber shampoo doesn't leave me unaffected. The warmth of her body is a call to mine and I can't help but react. There's this constant craving for her under my skin now that I've had her, and it's almost impossible to ignore when we're this close.

My right hand is still on her wrist, and I settle my left hand on her hip as she releases a small sigh.

"When you throw it, try to keep the rest of your body as still as possible. Don't squeeze the dart too hard in your hand."

"I know you're trying to help, but this is a little distracting." She looks over her shoulder at me and her eyes are half-lidded. She's clearly as affected by my proximity as I am hers.

"Want me to back up?"

"Don't you dare." She scowls at me then smiles.

"All right, give it a try and see what happens."

She raises her arm, lines up her shot, and… hits the wall beside the dartboard.

I laugh and step back.

"Some teacher you are," she grumbles but smiles.

"Do you want to try darts another night then?" I cover up my amusement by rubbing my palm over my mouth.

"I guess. I really wanted to tell the kids at school that I beat the burly football player at darts though."

I draw her into me, resting my hands on her lower back even though what I really want is to let them drop to her ass and give it a squeeze. "You can say you beat me. I won't tell anyone the truth."

She gives me a light punch in the bicep. "It's not the same."

"Well, is there something else you want to do then?" Twyla bites her bottom lip for a second and my dick twitches. "What is it, sunshine?"

She runs her palm over my pec, my shoulder, and down my arm. "I've been eyeing you in this shirt all night. You look really hot."

I arch an eyebrow. "Oh yeah?"

She nods. "Mmmhmm. This Henley fits you in all the right places and I've been thinking of ripping it off you since you showed up at my place earlier."

"I see. So what you're saying is that we should get back to your place immediately."

"Exactly."

I waste no time tugging her hand and leading her toward the exit. She laughs, and we say a quick goodbye to all the guys at the bar who normally just give me a grunt as a farewell. But because Twyla is with me, they look away from the TV and give a wave and a few words because they love her. Of course they love her. It only took a couple times of her being here with me for her to charm them all too.

We make it back to the condo building in record time, and as soon as the elevator doors close behind us and we're alone, I cage her in the corner.

"You have some good ideas." I lean into her, my hard length pressing against her.

She moans. "I do, don't I?"

Then we're kissing and she slips her hand between us and grips my length through my jeans. I push into her hand, wanting more.

This woman is my undoing. I want her more than my next breath.

We almost miss the sound of the elevator doors opening and it's only at the last second that she taps my shoulder, bringing me out of my daze. I turn and stab the door open button and the doors that were almost closed reverse and open.

Our hands are intertwined as we speed walk down the hallway to her door. Both of us are breathing fast while Twyla gets her key out to unlock the door. It's as if we're in a race— the adrenaline is high, as is the sense of urgency. And when she pushes open the door, I follow her in, slam it shut, then I'm on her.

I pick her up so her legs are wrapped around me and walk us into the living room while our tongues fight for supremacy. I win—I always do—and she lets me deepen the kiss, setting the pace.

When we reach the living room, I set her on the couch. It's

clear both of us are still eager for the other because we each undress ourselves. Within a minute, we're naked and I'm rolling the condom that was in my wallet down my shaft.

I grip the base and stroke myself as I look down at where she lies on the couch, naked and spread for me, one leg hooked over the back of the couch.

"You are the definition of temptation, woman." I drop to my knees in front of her.

My fingers dip between her legs and glide through her desire before I push two fingers into her. Her breathy moans hit my dick like a tuning fork and it becomes painfully hard, desperate for her wet heat.

I pump into her, arching my fingers and studying her every reaction, from the way her nipples peak into even sharper points and the way she grinds her hips, wanting more of me. Her breathing becomes shallower, and her eyelids are heavy. Every piece of this woman is cataloged in my brain so that I can retrieve it in the future after she's gone.

A growl rips out of my chest at the thought of this not being a part of my life anymore and I can't hold off any longer. I straighten, then hold my hand out to help her up. She stands and I lift her into the same position we were in when we arrived at the couch.

Her legs are wrapped around my waist, but I hook one arm, then the other, under the backs of her knees, keeping her spread open for me, and angle my hips so that I'm positioned at her entrance. I let gravity do its thing and she stretches around my cock until I'm fully seated inside her.

She moans and tosses her head back, her curly hair floating behind her. When I start moving, she straightens up and wraps her arms around my shoulders, turning her face into my neck. "Oh god, Chase."

I thrust my hips as I lift her on and off of my steel length. I feel myself bottoming out inside her. The pace grows more frantic as her short nails claw at my skin and her teeth lightly nip my neck.

"It feels so good," she moans. "It's so intense."

I love when she narrates what she's feeling for me. Her words give voice to what her body is already telling me.

When I change the angle of my hips slightly, she cries out with each and every drive of my cock and I know she's close. The slapping of our bodies and our heavy breathing are the only sounds in the quiet room and it sounds vulgar and messy, and damn if that doesn't ratchet my lust even higher.

Her pussy tightens around me. The next time I push inside her, her body goes rigid and shakes while she moans. She clenches around me and I slow the pace while she rides out her orgasm until she's limp in my arms.

We stand silent and still for a moment, then I turn around and lower myself to the couch. She sits astride me, and after a minute, she raises her head from my neck and meets my gaze. Her hair is sweaty and plastered to her face, so she pushes it away to get a clear view of me.

"That was unreal." Twyla looks at me with a mixture of disbelief and awe and places her hands on my face. "I didn't know it could be like that."

"Me either, sunshine." My voice is hoarse as I catch my breath.

She moves on top of me, our eyes still locked. I rest my hands on her hips but don't dictate the movement, letting her set the pace. She slides on and off, her nipples grazing my chest each time, but we don't look away from each other.

This is a world away from the frantic fucking we just did. This a one-eighty from two people who are attracted to each other just getting the lust out of their systems. This is something else entirely.

This is making love.

And though that scares the shit out of me, I'd never be able to stop even if I tried.

She rocks over me and I slide my hand into the hair at the side of her head. She leans into my touch, but we maintain eye contact. A kaleidoscope of pictures plays in her eyes— what already has and what could be in the future if we let it. Overwhelming emotion surges into my chest and I rock into her from below. I want so badly to kiss her, but I'm mesmerized by her eyes, unable to strip my gaze away.

Our breaths become labored, and when I move my other hand to where we're joined and circle her clit, she finishes with a breathy cry, arching her back, chin tilted toward the ceiling, eyes closed. Only then do I allow my own eyes to close, and I spill into the condom, body rigid.

I pull her to my chest, and she wraps her arms around my neck, head buried under my chin. Neither of us says a word while I let my fingertips brush her back, the both of us sensing the shift.

Now is when I could tell her how I feel or ask her what she sees happening when she has to leave. But for all my muscles and my bravado on the football field, I'm too chickenshit to bare my soul to this woman and ask her to give up everything she knows to stay here with me.

So, the feeling I gained while we made love is tempered by the feeling of loss that is yet to come.

twenty-five

. . .

Twyla

I pick up our clothes and follow Chase down the hall toward the room I've been staying in. It gives me an opportunity to check out his perfect, muscled ass. I didn't know I was an ass woman—I thought that was usually a guy thing—but there is absolutely nothing not to love about this man's derriere.

My legs wobble like Jell-O as I make my way into the bedroom. I can't even imagine how Chase's arms must feel. The fact that he has the strength to hold me for that long is a testament to the peak physical condition he's in.

I've just set the pile of clothes on the bed when the condo bell goes off and I hear the faint sound of someone knocking on the door.

Chase turns around, halfway into the bathroom, with a scowl. "You expecting someone?"

I shake my head. "No. Do you guys get solicitors in this building?"

"No, never. The concierge would never let them in."

With a frown, I walk toward the closet. "I should get it then. You stay here though, in case it's someone we know."

When I come back out of the closet wearing my robe, I can

tell that Chase doesn't like this idea. He's probably concerned for my safety or something equally sweet or protective, but we can't take the chance of him coming to the door with me when we don't know who it is.

"It'll be fine." I go up on my tippy-toes to give him a quick kiss.

He grumbles something as I make my way out of the room, shutting the door behind me.

The bell rings again and another knock sounds as I turn into the foyer. "Coming."

I take a quick peek out of the peephole on my tiptoes and mouth a soundless "Shit" when I see my brother standing there.

I whip the door open. "Miles, how did you get in the building?" I pull the top of my robe closed tighter as he walks past me into the condo.

"The concierge recognized me. Knows I'm here for Chase sometimes and that you've been living in the building." He turns to face me. "What's up? You just getting in the shower or something?"

"Uh… yeah. Exactly."

"Cool. I'll hang out until you're done." He walks into the living room and plops down on the couch, arms spread out behind him on the back of the couch.

"All right, but what are you doing here?"

That question sets off some type of brotherly radar because his head cocks to the side and he slowly gives me a once-over. "Thought I'd swing by and see if you wanted to hang out. Go get something to eat or whatever. Would have called, but I forgot my phone at home when I left to do errands."

I suck in a slow breath, attempting to relax my shoulders. "Oh, okay. Sure, just let me get ready real quick."

"I thought you were going to shower?"

"Yeah, that's what I mean. Just let me have a really quick

shower." I smile. "Do you want me to get you something to drink while you wait?"

"Don't suppose you have any protein drinks?"

I shake my head.

"All right, just a water then." He leans forward and grabs the remote for the TV off the coffee table while I head to the kitchen, wanting to get this over with so we can get out of there as fast as possible.

When I return to the living room, the TV is on, but Miles gives me a strange look. "Is someone else here? I thought I heard something down the hall."

I stiffen and shake my head. "Just the owner's cat."

His forehead wrinkles and he accepts the glass of water.

"I'll hurry and then we can leave."

"Yeah, okay." He turns his attention back to the TV.

I take off down the hall, trying not to appear as though I'm rushing when really, I feel like there's a poker an inch from my ass.

The moment I open the door to the master suite, Kiwi rushes out down the hall. Chase is standing there with his hands on his head, looking more stressed than I've ever seen him.

I quickly close the door and whisper, "What's with the look?"

"The damn cat went in the garbage and took out one of the condoms. I was chasing it around in here, trying to get the damn thing out of its mouth."

My eyes widen as adrenaline shoots through my system. "Oh my god, Miles is out there." I turn and rush down the hall, calling the cat's name. "Kiwi, come here, sweetie."

As soon as I reach the end of the hall though, I see my brother standing in front of the couch, staring at Kiwi. She's on the opposite side of the table, batting around the condom on the floor.

California could slide off into the ocean right now and it still wouldn't be enough to save me from my mortification.

"Is that what I think it is?" Miles says.

With a sigh and sagging shoulders, I step farther into the room. "It is."

Miles does an exaggerated full-body shiver as though it's the grossest thing he's ever seen, which… fair. I'd be the same had it been his condom.

"Why didn't you tell me you were seeing someone? Is he here?"

I put my hands on my hips. "I think it's pretty obvious why I didn't tell you. You would've grilled me about him, and I didn't want to deal with that. I didn't want the pressure of having to figure out what it all means because, let's be honest, that's what you'd demand to know."

He frowns. "You know I worry about you. Especially after—"

I raise my hand. "I know. Especially after Mathew, but look…" I raise my arms out at my sides. "I'm still here. It didn't break me."

"Is this your way of telling me I'm overprotective?" He arches an eyebrow.

"Just a bit." I give him a small smile.

He pulls me into a hug. "I'm sorry, sis. I just want the best for you. I'll try to back off."

I relax into his embrace. "Thank you, I'd appreciate that."

He pulls away and looks down at me, hands on my shoulders. "So who is this mystery man?"

I shake my head. "Nope. Once I figure out what is going on with us, then maybe I'll tell you."

He frowns, not liking my answer. But he must really be trying because he doesn't voice his displeasure. "Fair enough. Well, I think I'm going to skip that meal I suggested. I think I've lost my appetite after that." He nods behind him to where Kiwi is still messing around with the condom.

I chuckle, embarrassed still. "Next time, maybe call first."

He laughs. "Oh, believe me, I will not be showing up here again without an invitation."

He turns to leave, and I notice it at the same time as he does—a jacket that's half out, half under the side of the couch.

A jacket that only players of the San Francisco Kingsmen were issued. I know because my brother has an identical one.

I must have missed it when I was cleaning up our clothing.

Miles's eyes meet mine in disbelief. Before I can even open my mouth, he's stalking down the hallway toward the master suite.

"Miles, wait!" I call after him, but he's already at the door.

He whips it open, and his back stiffens. Chase stands in the middle of the room wearing just his underwear, looking shocked and a whole lot guilty. Miles steps inside and punches Chase in the face. My hands fly up to my mouth and I gasp.

Chase's face whips to the side, and when he straightens, he puts his finger in the air. "Consider that a freebie. Another one and it's game on."

I rush between them, my back to Chase while I push on Miles's chest. "Stop it!"

My brother doesn't even acknowledge me, and I can't budge him. I might as well be a feather between two boulders.

"My fucking sister?" my brother shouts. "You're supposed to be my friend. I asked you to look out for her and you take that to mean sleep with her?"

"Miles, back up." I push him again, and this time he relents, faltering back a couple of steps.

"I didn't want you to find out like this," Chase says, and although there's fury in his voice from being punched, the predominant tone is guilt.

Miles jabs his pointer finger at the air. "I can just imagine.

I'll bet you didn't ever want me to find out that you're fucking my little sister."

"Miles, calm down." I remain in front of Chase. Both men are pissed, but I know that neither of them would put me in harm's way.

"How long has this been going on?" my brother asks, then pushes both hands through the curls on top of his head. "Never mind, I don't even want to know. I have to get out of here." He spins around and leaves the bedroom.

I let him go. Now is obviously not the time to try to have a level-headed conversation about this.

After the door to the condo closes, I mutter, "I'll go get you some ice for your face."

I can't help but wonder if this will change things for us. There's no doubt that having to explain what's going on to my brother means we have to figure it out for ourselves first, something I think we've both been avoiding.

twenty-six

. . .

Chase

The locker room is tense upon our return after bye week, which isn't unusual given that the trade deadline is coming up so soon, but there's an extra layer of frost when Miles comes in and catches sight of me. He only looks at me briefly and says nothing.

I gave him a couple of days to cool off before I reached out to him, but he wouldn't answer my calls or texts. And when Twyla reached him, he picked up but said he was busy and would call her back later, but never did.

Lee and Brady exchange glances and look between us.

By now, they both know what went down. Miles must've left Twyla's and gone right to Lee's because Shayna called her that night. Then an hour later, Violet called. I have no idea if anyone else in the locker room knows, but I doubt it. Miles wouldn't go around advertising the fact that his sister is hooking up with one of his friends.

No part of betraying my friend's trust feels good, but more than that, the whole situation is upsetting Twyla and that's not okay with me. We need to figure this out so that Twyla's not in the middle.

I finish getting ready and hang around until most of the

other guys have left the locker room. Only then do I walk over to Miles.

"Can we talk for a second?" I ask.

He doesn't look up from where he's tying his shoes. "I don't know if it's a good idea."

My forehead wrinkles. "Why not? We need to sort this shit out."

"Because I don't want to be fined for fighting my own teammate in the locker room." He sits up.

"I get it, but it's hurting Twyla. I'll say what I need to say and you can say what you need to say and we go from there. How does that sound?"

Miles studies me for a moment then frowns. "Fine. Let's grab a beer after practice. Let's not do it here. I don't want other people up in my business."

I nod. "All right."

Miles walks past me, purposely brushing shoulders with me, but I let it pass. A part of me thinks I deserve it. But I can tell you one thing—if he tries to punch me again, it'll result in my second bar fight this season.

————

The waitress at the bar down the street from the stadium drops off our beers and stands for a beat with a flirty smile, waiting, I presume, to see if either of us will try to chat her up. When Miles and I continue to stare the other down silently, she leaves.

Miles takes a sip of his beer. I figure now is as good a time as any to start.

"I want to apologize for keeping it from you. I should've never agreed to lie to you about what was going on with me and your sister."

He raises an eyebrow. "What do you mean 'agreed'?"

I shift in my seat. I'm not trying to throw Twyla under the

bus, but I told myself that I would be honest about everything. "We had a discussion about it, and I let your sister make the decision. She didn't want to tell you." I sip my beer, waiting for him to answer.

"Jesus." He pushes a hand through his hair. "Am I really that much of an asshole that no one thinks they can tell me anything?"

My eyebrows draw down. "It's not that, but we all know how overprotective you are of your sister."

"I have my reasons," he grumbles.

"I know, the meningitis when she was a kid."

His head rears back. "She told you about that?"

I nod.

"She never tells anyone about that. It was such a difficult time in her life. We almost lost her and were so happy when she pulled through, only to have her be miserable at school for months afterward because her classmates were so vicious toward her for no reason."

"Kids are assholes."

A sad sort of chuckle leaves his lips. "That's for sure."

"My point is that it's a good thing she has you to look out for her, but she's a grown woman. You can't question every decision she makes, and I think that's why she didn't want to tell you. She knew you'd interrogate her about what was going on with us."

"And what exactly is going on with you two?" His voice is a little harder.

I sip my beer to buy myself a few seconds. "We haven't discussed the details."

He leans in. "Don't you think you should? Before someone gets hurt?"

"Believe me, I know I'm not good enough for your sister and I tried to stay away, I really did. But you know what she's like... she's like a sunbeam through the clouds after a month of rain. It's impossible not to be drawn into her."

Miles laughs, leaning back in his chair, hand on his stomach as though he can barely contain himself.

I scowl across the table. "What the hell is so funny?"

He shakes his head. "I've never heard you talk that way."

"What way?"

"Like a poet or some shit. You really like her, and I've never seen you fall for anyone before. It's weird. I figured you just grunted at your hookups for the most part."

Irritation bristles through me, but I decide to let it slide, given that I'm in the wrong for keeping all of this from him anyway. "Laugh it up. Like I said, I know she can do a hell of a lot better, but I'll take what I can get for the moment."

Miles sighs. "Maybe I was worried about the wrong person getting hurt." His sympathetic eyes make me want to punch him in the face.

Instead, I fist my hand on the table. "I knew when this started she'd be heading back to Connecticut."

"Yeah, but knowing it and dealing with it are two different things."

We sit there silently for a minute, both in our heads.

"At least you guys are using protection. I'd have to kill you if you knocked her up." He laughs.

"Fucking cat," I grumble, but we both laugh. When we're both done, I sober my expression and meet his gaze. "I really am sorry, Miles, but understand that I would never willingly hurt your sister."

He nods a few times. "Yeah, I know that. I was just shocked with how it all went down and a little hurt that neither of you told me. But I get it... I understand why it would've been hard to tell me."

"We good now?" My eyebrows rise.

"We're good." He stands from the table and I do the same, then we do the man-hug thing. When we pull apart, he claps me on the shoulder and says, "You should know though, she could do a hell of a lot worse than you, buddy."

I don't know what to say to that, so I say nothing. Luckily, Miles's phone rings on the table and we both take our seats.

He looks at the screen, then at me. "It's my agent Jagger. Mind if I take this for a second?"

"Not at all." I motion for him to answer the call.

"Hey, Jagger. How's it going?" Miles answers.

I can only hear Miles's side of the call, which consists of a lot of uh-huhs and okays, then his face goes blank and he says, "No shit, huh?" and finally, "All right." He hangs up, looking a little shell-shocked.

"Everything okay?" I ask.

He's staring at the table, still processing whatever he was told. "I just got traded to Chicago."

My first thought isn't about how I'll be sorry to see my friend go or how it will affect the team. My first thought is about how Twyla might feel about this and how, without Miles here, she won't have any real reason to visit San Francisco again.

twenty-seven

. . .

Twyla

The TV is on in the condo, but I haven't been watching it because I'm trying to read. I'm too nervous.

Chase texted me to let me know that he and Miles were going to grab a drink, and I've been a ball of anxiety, wondering if another fight will break out or whether they'll be able to repair their friendship. I've alternated trying to watch TV, pacing the living room, reading, and grooming Kiwi. None of it has been able to take my mind off what might be happening between my brother and my... my what? I don't even know.

We still haven't discussed what any of this means. Honestly, I think it's a topic we're both avoiding because we know I only have a few more weeks here until I have to return home. Kiwi's owner will be returning soon and my leave of absence at my job is expiring.

The writing is on the wall that whatever Chase and I have is due to end soon, but I'd be lying if I said that's what I want. When I jumped into this, I didn't do a lot of thinking about what might happen—I liked him, he treated me with respect, and he was hot as hell. But now it feels shortsighted of me to assume I wouldn't develop feelings for the man.

There's a knock at my door and I burst up off the couch and race down the hall. It must be Chase since the concierge didn't call up. I had words with him after the debacle that came from him letting my brother up unannounced that fateful day.

I whip open the door without looking to see who it is to find Chase *and* Miles standing there. That has to be a positive sign, right? As is the fact that neither of them looks as though they've punched the other. Chase still has a slight bruise on his face that I can sort of see through his short beard, but that's from when Miles hit him before.

"Hey, everything okay with you two?" I glance between them.

"Yeah," Chase says. "I'm gonna let you two talk, but I just wanted to be here when you opened the door so you'd know Miles and I are good." He kisses my forehead.

"We're good, but that's still weird, man," my brother says.

"It's a forehead kiss." Chase backs up and rolls his eyes. "Come see me when you guys are done."

There's something solemn about his voice that puts me on alert.

Chase claps my brother's shoulder. "See ya, man."

They do the man-hug thing, then Miles steps into the condo. It's then I realize the strain in his features.

"What's wrong? Is it Mom and Dad?" My stomach folds over on itself like a crepe.

"Mom and Dad are fine." He keeps walking until he's in the living room, then he takes a seat on the chair to the right of the couch. "Have a seat." He motions to the couch.

My stomach does cartwheels, but I do as he asks. "What's going on?"

He sighs. "I've been traded to Chicago."

I blink at him a few times as the information and all it means settles in my brain. "Chicago Grizzlies?"

He nods. "My agent called while I was out with Chase. Jagger insisted he be the one to tell me."

"Did you talk to Brady's parents? Why? Why would they do this?"

He nods again. "They called me on the way over. They're sad to see me go, but Chicago's desperate for a good safety and the offer was too good for them to turn down. It's a good trade for both teams." He sounds resigned but respectful of the decision.

"Did you see this coming at all?" I know a lot of players get jumpy around trade time, but Miles never said anything to me about the possibility.

"Not really. I mean, you know it's always a possibility and we have enough good safeties on the Kingsmen that they can stand to let one go. This is just how professional sports go sometimes."

I shuffle closer to the edge of the couch so I can take his hand. "How do you feel about this?"

He blows out a long breath. "Shocked mostly. I'm sad to leave all my teammates and I love this city, but I've never shied away from a challenge. Maybe the change will be good for me. Shake things up a bit." He smiles, but it doesn't reach his eyes.

It's clear to me that he's trying to put on a brave face, but he's still reeling from the decision. I squeeze his hand. "When do you leave?"

"Tomorrow morning." He meets my eyes and I see an apology in them.

"Wow, that fast?"

He nods slowly.

I let his hand go and flop back into the couch, thinking about how this affects me. My remaining few weeks here in San Francisco will be without my brother. I'll have no reason to come visit this city anymore, no reason unless...

No. I can't let my mind wander there. It will only lead to

disappointment. Chase has never said anything to me to make me think that his feelings run deeper than the two of us having a good time and enjoying each other's company.

"Which is why I wanted to make sure I came over here tonight to offer my apology in person."

I frown. "Apology? For what? I'm the one who was lying to you about Chase."

"For being so overprotective that you felt like you couldn't tell me in the first place."

"Miles—"

He raises his hand. "Let me just get this out. I've always felt like it's my job to look out for you since I'm six years older, especially after you got sick when we were young. But I never wanted to do it at the expense of us being able to be open and honest with each other."

My shoulders slump.

"I can see now that I need to let you live your life however you want to live it and just be a safe place for you to land if things go to shit. Not constantly trying to make sure you don't make any mistakes in the first place. I'm sorry if I've been overbearing at times."

My chest warms. I'm so lucky to have a brother who cares as much as he does, even if he doesn't know the best way to show it sometimes. "It's not just that I didn't want to tell you because I thought you'd be mad, Miles. I didn't know what to tell you. I don't know what any of this with Chase means. I have to return to my life in Connecticut in a few weeks."

"I can't say I know where Chase's head is at, but I can tell you this—I've never seen him spend any time or attention on a woman. Sure, I know he's had hookups over the years, but he never really talks about those women. I've certainly never seen him look the way he does when he talks about you."

"Which is how?" I hold my breath as I wait for him to answer.

"Like a man who's falling in love with a woman."

It's the answer I wanted to hear, but it doesn't fill me with the joy I thought it would since it's not coming from Chase.

"I don't know about that," I say quietly.

"I just know what I saw, but at the end of the day, it's up to you two to figure it out. I've already threatened him within an inch of his life that I'll bury him if he hurts you."

I chuckle. "You sure you're okay backing off on the protective big brother bit?"

He smiles and stands, holding his arms out to me for a hug. "That was my final duty before retirement."

I stand and hug him. "I hope everything works out for you in Chicago."

He pulls away and musses my hair. "Seems as good a place as any to finish out my career."

"I'll come visit once you're settled."

He nods. "I have some calls to make, so I gotta get going."

"Yeah, of course." I can't imagine how many people he wants to talk to before he goes, all the arrangements that need to be made. "If you need me to do anything at your place, just let me know. I still have my key."

I walk him to the door, and he gives me one last hug before he starts down the hall.

It's so weird to think that tomorrow he'll be in a different city and playing for a different team.

I watch until he gets into the elevator. He gives me a small wave before the doors close. After dipping inside my condo to grab my key, I lock up the place then knock on Chase's door.

The door whips open and a flood of emotions washes over me. I wrap my arms around Chase. One of his hands lands on the back of my head while the other gently rubs my back.

"How are you?" His deep voice rumbles in his chest against my ear.

"Sad, stressed for my brother, relieved the two of you made up."

181

"So a little of everything then?"

I hear the smile in his voice, and I look up at him. "I hope he likes it in Chicago."

The corners of his lips pinch together. "I'm sure he will once he gets settled. We'll miss him in San Francisco though."

Our eyes meet. It's on the tip of my tongue to ask what this means for us since I'll now have no real reason to return to the city, but I can't do it. I don't know where his head is, and I don't think I can take more rejection from someone I care about. Mathew did a number on me, but a part of me knows that if Chase tells me he has no interest in pursuing anything with me beyond the next few weeks that I'm here, then it will destroy me.

So instead of having the conversation we should have, I say, "Can we just cuddle on the couch tonight and watch our show to get my head off things?"

"Of course." He bends down and kisses my forehead.

It'll have to be a conversation for another day.

twenty-eight

. . .

Chase

It's been weird in the locker room without Miles there, and I know it's been weird for Twyla too. For the past week since Miles left, she's talked to him almost every day, checking in to see how he's doing.

There's also been a new tension between us. Nothing specific, but as her time in San Francisco draws nearer and nearer to coming to a close, I feel as though an elastic band is being pulled tighter and tighter. I haven't brought it up because I don't know what to say. Telling her I don't want things to end with her feels selfish. How could we possibly be happy living on the opposite side of the country from each other? Plus, she's so amazing that she deserves to be married to some Ivy League professor or something, not a guy who just barely made it through college.

I'm trying to keep in mind what's best for Twyla in the long run, not just thinking about what I want for myself. Because the truth is, I care enough about her that I'll gladly suffer and be miserable if it means she can be happier with someone else.

Earlier tonight we ordered dinner in, and we're halfway through a movie she wanted to watch—some rom-com about a couple who are supposed to have a destination wedding but the hotel gets taken over by pirates.

Tomorrow is game day for me, so I have an early bedtime. The past couple of weekends, Twyla has refused to stay over the night before a game because there's very little sleep that goes on if we're in bed together.

"I think I'm going to make some popcorn. Do you mind pausing the movie?" She sits up from where she was leaning into my side.

"Nope." I lean forward and hit Pause. "I don't have any here though."

She stands. "That's okay, I bought some microwave popcorn at the grocery store this week. I'll go make it at my place." Then she raises her hand. "And please don't tell me how terrible it is for me, I already know. Miles always harps on me about it when I eat it in front of him."

I chuckle. "No surprise there."

Miles is rigid with his diet and what he puts in his body. I eat pretty clean when the season is going on, but off-season, I can be a bit of a steak-and-potato guy. She won't be getting any lectures from me.

Before she makes it to the door, her phone rings. She stops, pulls it out of her back pocket, and stills. I can tell by the look on her face that whoever it is, she's either not happy about it or not expecting their call. She continues out the door and I hear her say hello in the hallway before the door closes.

"Who the hell is that?" I say to Zeus who is curled up in the cat bed Twyla insisted he needed.

He raises his head and looks at me, then lowers it again and closes his eyes.

"A lot of help you are," I grumble. I remind myself that it's none of my business.

But I don't even have to pry about who was on the phone when Twyla returns a couple of minutes later—no popcorn in hand—because she takes a seat on the opposite end of the couch. "That was Mathew on the phone."

I grind my teeth. "Do I need to have another conversation with him?"

"He's here, in San Francisco. Apparently he flew out here to see me since I wouldn't return any of his calls or texts."

I want to pound this guy into the ground. And then I remind myself that I have no right. It's not like Twyla's my girlfriend or has even told me how she feels about me.

"Why aren't you saying anything?" she asks a little hesitantly.

"What do you want me to say?"

"I'm not sure, really. I don't know what to do."

"You mean you're actually thinking of meeting him?"

She shrugs. "I don't know. Maybe I should."

That does it for me. No need to ask how she's feeling about us. The fact that she's entertaining the idea of meeting her ex-fiancé says it all.

Then I realize that maybe this is a good thing. Maybe this is exactly what we need to make a clean break of things before she leaves.

"Well, then… maybe you should go see what he has to say." I barely get the words out. They feel like sandpaper on my tongue.

She stares at me for a beat then nods. "Yeah, maybe I will."

"Great, it's decided then." I reach for the remote and press Start on the movie again.

"You know what? I'm beat. I think I'm going to go back to my place and read for a bit then go to bed."

I click Pause and stand when she does. "Yeah, okay."

I follow her to the door, and when she opens it, we stand there somewhat awkwardly. She gives me a small wave at the same time that I bend to kiss her cheek and it's uncomfortable and awkward and just all-around awful. Normally we'd be making out at my door, me trying to convince her to stay while she tells me it's better for me if she leaves.

It's a struggle not to tell her to ditch Mathew, that I'm jealous and I don't want her meeting up with him, but I can't do it. I've never had a serious relationship, and I'm terrified to tell Twyla how I feel about her. What if she doesn't feel the same? What if I am just some fun she is having before she goes and tries to find someone else to settle down with? And all signs point to that being the reality of the situation.

I'm already going to walk away from this with a broken heart. I'd like to retain some pride at least.

"Good luck at the game tomorrow." She gives me a small smile that doesn't light up her eyes the way it normally does.

"Thanks. You still coming even though Miles won't be there?" I told her earlier in the week that I'd leave her a ticket at will call.

"Not sure. We'll see."

My jaw clenches, but I force it to relax. "All right then."

"See you later, Chase." She walks across the hall to her condo and gives me one last look before she goes inside and closes the door.

I don't know if it would be better or worse if that were the last time I saw her.

———

The moment I wake up the next morning, I feel like I have made a mistake.

Even if Twyla doesn't see me as more than a fling, there's no way she should be with someone who broke off their engagement because he fell for someone else. She deserves better than that.

I hurry and get ready, gathering my things for the game faster than normal so that I'll have some extra time to talk to Twyla before I leave.

Once I'm ready, I head across the hall and stand in front of her door with my hand raised… and I hesitate.

Shit.

Is this the right thing to do or am I leading her on?

With a muffled curse, I turn and head down the hall. I only make it halfway before circling back and knocking on her door. I wait then ring the bell, followed by another knock, but she doesn't answer.

My heart feels as if it's part of that Plinko game on *The Price Is Right* and it's just ricocheting down through metal spikes in different directions until it hits the ground. I trudge toward the elevator with sunken shoulders, staring at the floor.

Has she already gone to meet Mathew?

Did I screw up an opportunity at the best thing I've ever had?

twenty-nine

. . .

Twyla

I sit on a bench in Golden Gate Park, waiting for Mathew to arrive, and think back to last night.

When I picked up his call, it was with the full intention of telling him to go to hell and to stop calling me. But when he blurted out that he'd flown all the way out here to talk to me, I felt a certain sense of... responsibility? Guilt? I'm not sure. But I felt like I should at least hear him out.

Not for his sake. For mine.

Now that enough time has passed since he called things off and I'm not as emotional about the situation, there are things I want to say to him. Things I couldn't say when all of this first went down.

Still, Chase doesn't know that. For all he knows, I'm here to reconcile with Mathew. The fact that it didn't seem to bother him one bit hurt more than it probably should have, given that we both knew this was bound to be over in a little more than a week.

I wanted him to ask me to stay, tell me not to go because he was afraid he'd lose me. I wanted to be someone's choice for once, but I couldn't say that, not after what Mathew did. I couldn't take the rejection. I'd hoped we were building something, but I guess I was the only one.

Chase is quiet and unassuming and, yes, super grumpy if you don't know him, but one thing he isn't is a bullshitter. So if he says he doesn't care if I meet Mathew, I know he means it. Even if I wish he didn't.

It's a fairly nice day, and I watch families walk by with their kids. One of the dads is wearing a Kingsmen hat and it makes my heart pinch. I wonder how long that will happen. Will I feel like bursting into tears every time I see a sports report that mentions the Kingsmen, or will I want to turn away if I see Chase's jersey on someone else's back?

Mathew catches me by surprise when he sits down beside me because I'm so deep in thought.

"Hey, thanks for meeting me."

My gaze settles on him and… nothing.

Gone is the longing I felt whenever I looked at a picture of him on my phone. Gone is the hurt that pinched my chest when I saw his name on my phone. Gone is the betrayal that burned in the pit of my stomach when I remembered the day he told me it was over.

It's all just… gone.

And god, is that a relief.

"I wasn't sure I was going to, but you came a long way." My voice is colder than he's used to.

He seems to pick up on that, swallowing hard. "You didn't leave me much choice."

"Why are you here, Mathew?" I'm not going to sit here and let him try to make me feel bad about not wanting to speak to him after what he did.

He frowns. "I miss you."

I garner no reaction. "What do you want me to say to that?"

"Well, I'm hoping that you miss me too." He glances at a couple walking past and holding hands.

"Even if I did—which I don't anymore—what would the difference be? You already ruined what we had together. There's no coming back from that."

He sighs and his shoulders turn inward. "I know I fucked up. I know. I was feeling the pressure of the wedding and the planning and how much everything was going to cost, and I let myself get caught up in something that seemed easy."

"Seemed?"

"Rachel and I aren't together anymore. I broke it off when I realized I'd made a horrible mistake. I could never love her the way I love you."

I shake my head. "It's almost as if you think that's a compliment."

"If it makes a difference, I didn't sleep with her until after we broke up," he says, looking a little more desperate. He must have thought he'd waltz in here and I would take him back after a little bit of groveling.

A caustic laugh leaves my lips. "Even if I believed that was true, it wouldn't matter. You still betrayed me, and honestly, that's what hurt the most. That after all the years we spent together, you couldn't just tell me that the wedding was getting to you, or that you wanted to slow things down, or that you didn't feel the same way about me, whatever. Instead, you pursued something with someone else and made me feel like I wasn't good enough. But the truth is that you're not good enough for me, Mathew. So no, I won't be taking you back. There's nothing you can do to explain away the pain you caused me."

His eyes narrow and his cheeks turn red. "So what? Is this because you're with that football player now?"

"Not that it's any of your business, but I'm not with him. And even if I were, it wouldn't matter. There's no universe in which you and I get back together."

"I flew all the way out here." He sounds irritated now that he knows it was a wasted effort.

"I'm sorry it didn't work out how you planned, but there's something else I wanted to tell you." I stand from the bench and turn to face him. "I expect you to pay my parents back for the deposits they couldn't get refunded, and if you refuse, I'll take you to court. You're the one who led me on and broke off our relationship well after you knew my parents would still be responsible for that money, so you're responsible. I'm not going to clean up your mess. You need to."

His mouth drops open and he looks as though he wants to argue.

Stabbing a finger in his direction, I say, "If our time together meant anything at all to you, and if you really mean what you said when you came here today, you'll do this. It won't change my mind about getting back together, but it is the ethical thing to do."

His lips press into a thin line, and he gives a jerky nod. "Fine."

"Thank you." I let out a relieved breath. I would have gladly paid my parents back, but it feels good not to have to worry about it.

Mathew leans forward, resting his elbows on his knees, and pushes his hands through his hair, staring at the ground. "I'm sorry I messed everything up."

He sounds upset and depressed, and I fight the urge to console him. Not because I have loving feelings for him anymore, but because I don't like seeing anyone upset.

I sit beside him on the bench again. "I guess the best you can do now is learn from it. Next time you're in a relationship, talk to her about how you're feeling. Even if it's an uncomfortable conversation. Don't let things fester under the surface. That's when bad decisions are made."

The truth of my words rings through my head and I realize that I should have taken my own advice. I should've told Chase how I felt and brought up my impending departure and asked how he saw it playing out. Instead, I was so

Piper Rayne

afraid of being rejected that I stayed silent. The same way I did in my relationship with Mathew when I had my first inkling that something could possibly be amiss.

"I'm an idiot," I mumble, but Mathew turns toward me.

"What?"

"Nothing." I wave him off. There's nothing I can do about my realization now. Chase was okay with me seeing Mathew, which tells me where he stands. In the future, I'll always speak about what I want without worrying about getting my heart broken. "Take care of yourself, Mathew. I hope you find happiness with someone and know how to hang on to it."

We stand from the bench and give each other a hug. This man brought me a lot of pain, but I can honestly say that this time away from him and my time with Chase has given me a newfound perspective. I no longer yearn for what might have been with Mathew.

Now I yearn for what I know I'd be missing with Chase.

thirty

. . .

Chase

By the time I reach the locker room, I know I messed up. And when I step out onto the field and don't see Twyla sitting in the wives and girlfriends' section, the knowledge that she could be with Mathew right now, taking him back, sits like a boulder in my stomach.

My head isn't in the game. I should have been the one traded if you go by my performance.

Thank God my teammates' heads are though. We end up winning by a small margin.

I can't get off that field fast enough, and when I return to the locker room, I don't talk to anyone, quickly getting undressed, showered, and over to the media room to do my mandatory postgame interview so that I can get the hell out of here and see if Twyla's back at her condo yet.

I don't even know what I'm going to say to her. I'm just desperate to see her, to know if she forgave that sack-of-shit Mathew and is entertaining the idea of getting back together with him.

But when I'm done with my interview—which mostly consisted of a bunch of glares and grunts from me when the media, rightly so, called me out on my shitty performance today—Lee and Brady are standing in the hallway, seemingly waiting for me.

"What's up?" I ask when they share a look then look back at me.

"We've both gotta do our interviews, but then let's head back to Brady's place," Lee says.

I shake my head. "I got somewhere I gotta be."

Brady nods as though expecting my answer. "We know, but you can't go see her without a plan, man."

My eyes narrow. "What are you talking about?" I cross my arms and stare down my nose at him.

"Look, we both know the signs... you fucked up in some way," Brady says.

"We've both been there." Lee shrugs.

Brady counts his points off on his fingers. "You're pissier than usual, your head wasn't in the game, you look like you lost your best friend, you're..." He trails off when he sees the look I'm giving him, then raises his hands. "It's nothing to be ashamed of. Lee and I have been there. Now it's our turn to help you with your grand gesture."

"I don't need a grand gesture," I grumble, not really believing my words.

Lee claps me on the shoulder. "You always need a grand gesture when you screw up large. You read that romance book, so surely you must know that."

I roll my eyes. He's right though. It worked for Lee and Brady when they messed up royally with Shayna and Violet.

"Fine. I'll meet you at your place." I don't let them say anything else, instead pushing past them to head back to the locker room to grab my stuff.

They were able to win their girls back. I can only hope I'll be able to do the same.

———

A couple hours later, we're seated in Brady's living room, nursing some beers, when Violet brings in Brady's laptop.

"Here you go." She sets it on the coffee table and swings her gaze my way briefly before straightening.

I want badly to ask what, if anything, Twyla has said to her about me, but I don't want to put her in an uncomfortable position.

"Thanks, babe." Brady gives her hand a brief squeeze.

"I'm going to take Theo to the park so that you guys can have some privacy," she says.

"Sounds good, thanks."

Once Violet and Theo are out of the house, both guys turn their attention to me.

"I'm gonna loop Miles in on a video chat so he can chime in on this too," Brady says.

I groan and push a hand through my hair. "Really? You think that's necessary?"

"Of course it is. You and Miles are good now, and who better than her brother to tell you how to get back on her good side?"

He has a point, as much as I wish he didn't. "Fine," I grumble.

Brady does his thing on his laptop and patches Miles in on a video call, setting the laptop on the coffee table. I get up off the chair and walk around to sit in the middle of the couch between Lee and Brady.

"Hey, man," I say when he comes on-screen. I feel as though an extra layer of guilt has been painted on my skin.

"Look at you three. This must be serious," he says good-naturedly.

I whip my head to my right to look at Brady. "You didn't tell him why we're calling?"

"Nah, I figured you could do that." He shrugs.

I groan and tip my head back, scrubbing my hands over my face.

"How's Chicago?" Lee asks.

"They have me in a short-term rental right now that's pretty sweet, so I can't complain about that. But there's a cold snap happening right now. I forgot what fall's like when you're not in California."

Lee and Brady chuckle, but I can't be bothered because, in seconds, I'm going to have to tell Miles that I did the one thing he warned me not to—hurt his little sister.

"So, what's up?" Miles asks.

In my peripheral vision, I see Lee and Brady turn to look at me.

I sigh. "I messed up and hurt Twyla."

Miles's jaw flexes. I wait for him to lay into me, but it doesn't come.

"What happened?" he asks.

I explain how things have been a little tense since he left and how I think it was because Twyla and I never discussed what would happen when she had to leave. Then I tell him about Mathew's call and how I didn't discourage her from going to see that idiot.

"You didn't tell her to send him packing back to Connecticut?" This is the first time Miles interrupts me.

"I know, it was stupid. I knocked on her door this morning to try to take it back, but she wasn't there. I think she'd probably already left to go meet him."

"What the hell were you thinking?" Miles asks.

"I don't know what I was thinking!" I throw my hands up in front of me. "I was thinking she could do better than me and that she deserves someone who can give her his full attention all the time, not a guy who will have to make her number two on his priority list for half the year during football season. She's so bubbly and I hate talking."

"Not right now. You're a fucking chatterbox." Brady snickers.

"Has Twyla seemed unhappy with what you're able to give her since she's been here?" Lee asks.

"No, I guess not," I grumble. "We don't even live in the same city or on the same side of the country. Her life is in Connecticut. I don't have the option to just uproot my life and move to the East Coast to be with her."

"Admittedly, that's a problem," Miles says. "But Twyla has been able to visit me all the time. Or maybe she'd be willing to move there. You owe her a conversation at least."

I'm quiet for a minute, looking at my hands before I look back up at Miles. "What if she moves here to be with me, leaves everyone and everything she knows, and I fuck it up?"

"Why are you so sure you're gonna mess it up?" Brady asks.

"I don't know anything about relationships. I've never been in a serious relationship before. I'm grumpy and like being alone a lot of the time. I don't enjoy being social and being around a lot of people and God knows Twyla thrives in that kind of environment. What if I can't make her happy?"

"Why are you so sure you can't?" Lee says.

"You can just say it," Miles says through the laptop.

I turn my attention that way. "Say what?"

"That you're scared."

I give him a deadly look, but my mouth doesn't open to argue with him because it's the truth. "I couldn't live with myself if I hurt her."

"But you're already hurting her because you're not being honest with her about how you feel," Brady says.

"What if she moves here and I get traded? Look at Miles." I gesture to him on the screen. "He had less than a day's notice before he had to pick up his life and move. She'd have to pick up her life and start all over again in another new city."

"You can come up with all the excuses you want, but I

think what it really comes down to is how you feel about her. Do you love her?" Miles asks.

My heart rate picks up speed and the hairs on the back of my neck stand on end. I already know the answer—have known it for a while. I do love Twyla. But saying the words requires a certain type of vulnerability I'm not used to sharing with anyone. It feels as though if I say them, I'll be handing the power to destroy me over to someone else.

As if he can read my thoughts, Lee says, "Whether you say it or not, the reality remains the same."

"Yeah, Lee and I both know how hard it is to put yourself out there and risk it, but trust us when we say that it's so much better once you're on the other side of that." Brady claps a hand on my shoulder.

"All right, fine. I love her." I give Miles an "Are you happy?" look.

He laughs as if it's the funniest thing he's ever heard. "I know I wasn't happy about it when I first found out, but honestly, I know what kind of man you are and I know you'll put her happiness first, Chase."

Brady claps his hands in front of him. "Now we just have to figure out what Chase's grand gesture is going to be."

"You're gonna hate it, whatever it is," Lee says.

"It's going to force you outside of your box," Miles says.

"Whatever it takes. If it means I get to be with Twyla, it's worth it."

And as we come up with the plan, I remind myself of those words a thousand times because this is one hundred percent out of my comfort zone.

thirty-one

. . .

Twyla

It's my last Sunday in San Francisco before the owner of the condo returns and I must go back to my life in Connecticut. The prospect makes me sad because, for a while, I felt as though I was building a new life here in California.

I haven't seen Chase this week. Whether that's by design or fate, I'm not sure, but a part of me is sad and disappointed that he hasn't reached out. Sure, I could have gone across the hall and knocked on his door, but what would be the point? The fact that he hasn't tried to talk to me tells me everything I already knew when he told me to go meet Mathew.

The Kingsmen have a game today, and after much persistence on her part, I agreed to watch the game with Violet in the owner's box. She reasoned that it would probably be the last time I'll get to see her, Bryce, and Shayna before I leave. The unspoken part was that with Miles not playing for the Kingsmen anymore, we really don't know when I'll see them again.

My time here was successful at getting me to move on from my feelings about Mathew, but as my departure draws nearer, I realize that I'm leaving more heartbroken than I arrived. It's just over a different man.

Chase burrowed his way into my heart and there's no way I'll ever get him out.

Which is why I'm so nervous as I make my way up to the owner's box at the stadium. I won't have to see Chase face to face in person today, but I'll have to watch him play and that feels almost as bad. To know that we'll be existing in the same space and yet won't be interacting at all other than as complete strangers… it feels like a hot poker in my chest.

But I put on a brave face and a smile as I walk through the door to the owner's suite.

"Twyla, you made it!" Brady's mom, Lennon, is the first to spot me. I met her at the gala and let's just say that she is a handful.

I can't imagine growing up with Lennon as a mom. When I think of my ultraconservative mom saying some of the things that come out of Lennon's mouth, I could dissolve into a fit of giggles.

"Hi, Mrs—" I stop myself. She made it clear at the gala that she prefers to be called by her first name. "Hi, Lennon."

"So glad you could come, sweetie. I heard you'll be heading back to the East Coast soon?" She frowns.

I nod. "Yeah, in a few days."

"And what's this I hear about you and a certain number seventeen?" Her eyebrows rise in interest.

"Oh, um… we're not really a thing anymore." My cheeks heat.

How the hell does she know anything about Chase and me?

She eyes me appraisingly. "These things have a way of working out. I saw you two together at the gala. That's not likely something that's going to fizzle out. Trust me." She leans in and winks as though we're sharing a secret.

"Oh no, that wasn't a real date. I was just his plus-one." I look over her shoulder for someone, anyone, to save me from this uncomfortable conversation and spot Violet, who glances up from talking to Theo and does a double take, eyes widening.

"That might've been the story you both told yourself, but I have a keen eye for this sort of thing. It'll all work out." She squeezes my hand.

"Hey, Twyla. How long have you been here?" Violet gives me a knowing look as she comes up behind Lennon.

"Just a minute. Thanks again for having me."

Lennon waves off my thanks. "I'm sorry we couldn't keep your brother here, but you're always welcome regardless."

I smile as Violet loops her arm through mine. "Come see Theo. He's been asking when you'd get here." Before Lennon can say anything, she spins us and walks us to the far side of the room. "Sorry, I didn't see you come in," she whispers. "Was she already grilling you about your sex life?"

I chuckle. "I think we were just warming up to that part."

"Thank God I saved you then."

Theo rushes up to say hello to me. He's pretty comfortable with me now that I see him a bit at school throughout the week. The school is just another thing I'll be sad to leave. They have a really good community there.

I chat with Violet and Theo for a bit, then say hello to Brady's dad, Jasper, and some other people in the room. Bryce pops by from the press box for a bit before she has to return since the game will be starting soon.

I'm standing by myself behind the top row of seats, looking out into the stadium full of fans and feeling a little melancholy. I had a lot of fun here watching my brother play and then watching Chase play, and not knowing whether I'll ever be back just feels off.

I'm deep in thought when a voice comes on over the sound system in the arena. I look at the screen high above the stadium and startle when Chase's face fills the entire screen.

He's dressed and ready for the game, but he doesn't have his helmet on. I'm not sure what's going on. Is he a part of some ceremony before the game starts or something? Did he reach some milestone in his career I'm not aware of and is getting an award?

But when he opens his mouth and the first thing that comes out of it is my name, I know it has nothing to do with that.

"Twyla, I fucked up and I'm sorry," he says.

"I told him no cursing," Mr. Banks says somewhere from behind me and I realize that probably everyone in this room is in on this.

Chase is walking, but I don't realize where until I see myself on the enormous screen, Chase standing behind me. I whip around, hands over my mouth and tears in my eyes.

"Twyla, I've never been good at expressing my feelings. When my dad died, I didn't even cry. I never talked to anyone about how I was feeling, even though my insides felt like they were being shredded. It seemed easier to just push all that shit down and hope it would go away someday." He gently coasts his fingertips down my cheek.

Something about such a large, powerful man being so careful with me is my undoing and one tear drips down my face.

"Don't worry, this isn't being televised, sunshine. Though I'm pretty sure it'll be up on YouTube in minutes."

I follow his gaze down into the stadium where thousands of people have their phones pointed up at the screen. A watery laugh leaves my lips.

"I may not be good with my words, but I like to think my actions with you have shown you how I feel about you. Your needs are above my own and I'll do anything I can to make you happy. I realize that you need to hear the words and actions alone aren't enough."

I think about what he's saying and remember him

showing me his Lego room and taking me to his favorite spot in the city—The Crooked Nail—the night of my would-be wedding. How he couldn't bring himself to give up Zeus and how he pulled me into his lap the night I was so scared when we were watching *American Horror Story*. How he didn't hesitate to stick up for me with those guys in the bar even though it could have been front page news and hurt his career. How he told Mathew to go to hell when he kept calling. The way he opened up to me about his dad's death and how hard it was for him.

He's right. He may not have been professing his love for me out loud, but he's been showing me all along exactly how he feels.

"But you didn't care if I went to see Mathew." My voice echoes throughout the stadium and it's jarring.

He pushes a hand through his hair. "I was an idiot. I thought you were better off without me and that was just a means to an end to cut ties. I've been a mess since you walked out that door."

Irritation fizzes in my blood. "You're no different than my brother, thinking you know what's best for me rather than letting me decide what I want."

He nods. "I realize that now. You're one-hundred-percent right, but I like to think that I learn from my mistakes and it's not one I'll make again."

I study his face, see the sincerity there, and I believe him.

He puts the mic down on the table and takes my hands. Lennon picks it up and hovers it by us. "Please stay. Or go if you have to and we'll figure it out somehow. But I want you with me. I want to come home to you and go to bed with you and wake up with you. I want you, me, and Zeus to be a unit, a family, and eventually, I want to start our own."

I suck in a sharp breath. If I stay now, it's one hundred percent for Chase. My brother is no longer in San Francisco. I'd be uprooting my life and putting all of my eggs in Chase's basket. In the gamble that we can be happy together and make it long term.

"I love you, Twyla. And I fully intend to marry you one day, though I don't plan to ask you in such a public fashion. This is a one-off to prove to you that I mean every word I say."

My lips quiver as I stare into the soulful brown eyes of the man I cannot live without.

This must be painful for him. Chase is not a man who loves the spotlight. He's private and not good at expressing his emotions, so doing so in such a public way is a sacrifice he's made to show me how much he means it.

My chest fills with joy, and I feel as if I could burst. "I love you too."

His hands come to my face, and he bends to kiss me. When our tongues meet, it's as if all of the tension from the past weeks slides out of me, down through my toes and into a puddle on the floor.

He pulls away and rests his forehead on mine. "Does that mean you'll stay?"

I nod slowly. "Of course I'll stay."

Chase kisses me again, and when he pulls away, he winks at me. "It's the muscles, isn't it?"

We both dissolve into a fit of laughter while the crowd in the stadium goes wild and the people around us offer us their good wishes.

After a minute or two, Jasper approaches and says to us, "Congratulations, you two. Well done, Chase."

Chase shakes his hand. "Thanks, Jasper."

"Now, get out there and get us a win." He nods toward the field.

"Will do." Chase turns to me. "I'll see you downstairs after the game."

"Try and stop me." I smile as he leans in to give me a chaste kiss.

I head back to where I was standing when he showed up, and I smile to myself.

I'd thought it was the start of a whole new life when I arrived here three months ago, but today is the real start to my whole new life.

epilogue

. . .

Twyla

I'm at the kitchen sink, rinsing out the glass I used for orange juice when a large set of hands settles on my hips. Chase leans down and kisses my neck and a little moan escapes me.

"Good morning," he says against my skin.

"Morning."

"How'd you sleep?" he asks before kissing my temple.

"Hmm, not well. I couldn't keep my hands off my boyfriend all night, so there wasn't much sleep to be had."

He chuckles in my ear. "Must be the muscles that make him so irresistible."

"Always blame the muscles," I say in a breathy voice when he steps into me so that his body is plastered against mine.

"Knock it off, you two." Miles steps into the kitchen and heads to the fridge for one of his green drinks.

Chase laughs and steps back from me, adjusting himself.

We're in Chicago, visiting my brother, although Miles decided to keep his place in California so that he could spend time there during the off-season and be around me and his friends from his old team. Training camp starts next week, so Miles has already returned to his rental condo in Chicago, and we decided to come have a quick visit here before Chase is to report to the Kingsmen training camp.

I ended up getting a teaching job at the same school I was helping out at, so I'm off on summer break, which works out well.

This is our second time visiting my brother in Chicago and we're here to see him, yes, but I also have two other reasons to be here that Miles doesn't know about yet. One of which I'm afraid to tell him.

Miles takes his disgusting-looking green drink from the fridge and swallows it, making my stomach turn.

"I don't know how you drink that stuff." A full-body shiver works its way through me.

"I don't know how you eat all the processed crap you put in your body," he says back.

I stick my tongue out at him like an adolescent.

"All right, children, settle down," Chase says.

"I love your dad voice," I say to my boyfriend, and we share a knowing smile.

"If you tell me you call him daddy in the sack, I might puke," Miles says.

"Not in the bedroom, but you're giving me ideas..." I rest my index finger on my chin and look at the ceiling, then break into a laugh.

"Speaking of..." Chase gives me a look that says, "get on with it."

We've been here for two days and still haven't told my brother the news. Either one. I've chickened out every time, but Chase is clearly done giving me a free pass.

"What?" Miles looks between the two of us.

"Why don't you sit down?" I gesture to the large island in the middle of the kitchen.

Miles has a wary look on his face as he sits. "Okay, what's going on?"

Chase stands behind me, resting his chin on my head, his hands on my waist.

"We have some news."

Miles's gaze dips down to my bare left hand.

I continue, "We wanted you to be the first to know since you were so out of the loop on the first bit of news we had when we got together."

Miles's eyes narrow. He's fine with Chase and I being a couple now, but he's still a little bitter about how he found out.

"Chase and I are expecting a baby. I'm pregnant."

Chase's hand roams from my waist to my belly and he kisses the top of my head.

Miles stares at us in shock for a moment, and my breath catches. Will he not be happy about this news?

Then he snaps out of it, pushes out of his seat, and walks around the island, arms outstretched. "Congratulations! Oh my god, I'm going to be an uncle."

His smile is wide as he pulls me into a hug, squeezing tightly.

"Careful there, man," Chase grumbles behind me.

Chase has been even more protective than normal since he found out I was pregnant. Not in an overbearing way, in a sweet, loving way. He won't let me carry anything that could be considered remotely heavy, and he won't let me clean the kitty litter because he read somewhere that there's a small chance it could make me or the baby sick, and he's constantly massaging my feet even though I just passed over the twelve-week mark.

I was only nervous to tell Chase I thought I might be pregnant for about the length of a heartbeat. Once I wrapped my own head around the idea, I wasn't worried about what he would think—I knew he'd stick by me and be down for whatever the future had in store for us.

We took the test together, and when he saw the two lines appear, I saw a mix of awe and elation on his face.

Miles pulls away from me, then he and Chase hug, but not in that bro way guys do. A real honest-to-goodness hug. I'd be lying if I said I didn't want to snap a picture and send it to all the girls. It's not every day you see two hulking football players let their guard down and embrace.

"I wasn't sure how you'd react," I say once he and Chase separate.

"Really?" Miles's forehead wrinkles. "Of course I'm happy for you. And if you thought I was an overprotective brother, you just wait and see what I'm like as an uncle." He winks and laughs.

I thumb at Chase beside me. "I think you'll have to compete with this one for the designation of most protective."

Chase grumbles something I can't hear, but I'm only teasing. I can't wait to see his protective instincts encompass our child.

"So does this mean a wedding is coming in the next few months?" Miles asks.

I shake my head. "We talked about it, but we decided we'd rather wait until we're settled as a family after the baby has arrived. We're not in any rush."

Miles looks at Chase. "You do plan on marrying her, right?"

"Relax, big brother. I tried to get her to dip down to city hall with me, but she refused. I'd marry her in a heartbeat, but I don't need a ring on my finger to know what I got." He hooks his arm around my side and pulls me in, kissing my temple.

I shrug. "The first time around, I was going to get married, then do the family thing, and look how that turned out. Right now, I just want to concentrate on getting ready for this baby." My hand skims down over my tummy and I look up at Chase. "I know neither of us is going anywhere."

"You can say that again." He smiles down at me.

"Except for me. Right now. I have to pop out and meet someone." I pull away from Chase and look at my brother, sucking in a deep breath. This is the part I was most nervous to tell him.

Miles gives me the once-over. "I was wondering why you were already dressed and ready to go. Who are you meeting?"

"Um… I'm just going to help someone with something for the day."

Miles frowns. "I didn't realize you knew anyone in Chicago. Except for me."

"Well… I didn't. They're new here too."

Chase chuckles. "Just tell him, sunshine."

Miles stills. "Tell me what?"

I shift in place. "Bryce got a job at *Sportsverse Magazine* and their head office is here in Chicago, so she just moved here. I'm helping her unpack and get organized at her new place."

My brother blinks a few times, slowly. "Bryce lives in Chicago now?"

I nod. "Yep. But it's a big city. I'm sure you guys won't even see each other."

I give Miles what I hope is an encouraging smile. I still don't know what the deal is between those two, but I'm certain it's more than the line each of them has given us— "we're just too different" or "we just don't like each other."

When he still doesn't move, I say, "Miles, say something." It's like he's gone catatonic.

He snaps out of it, giving his head a shake. "You're right, it's a big city. I'll never even see her. It's not gonna be a problem."

But something in my gut, call it newfound motherly intuition, says that he's one-hundred-percent wrong about that. I guess only the future will tell.

The End

cockamamie unicorn ramblings

Well, the Kingsmen Football Star series is over. But we're not done with football, not by a long shot!

This series was a lot of fun to write though admittedly Piper had to do some brushing up on her football. While she was a pro at scrolling TikTok and watching hot football player videos, she was not that acquainted with the game itself. LOL

One reason we loved writing this story is because we always love a grumpy/sunshine set-up, and it was interesting to explore Chase as a character. He was pretty quiet the first couple of books, but we knew that underneath that grumpy exterior, there was a protective teddy bear just waiting for the right girl!

If you're wondering who the inspiration for Chase was, you can google Nick Bosa and thank us later. ;)

As far as the writing went not much changed in this one from conception to the final product. Some books are easy to write, and others are a struggle and this one was honestly just a pleasure. We had to force ourselves to make Chase and Twyla leave his apartment because we enjoyed writing their interactions so much that it didn't matter where they were. LOL

I think the scene where Chase is hosting Brady and Violet's engagement party was one of the most fun ones we've written in this series. Looking at that entire situation through the lens of a brooding football player was amusing, to say the least. LOL

As always, we have a lot of people to thank for getting this book into your hands!

Nina and the entire Valentine PR team.
Cassie from Joy Editing for line edits.
Ellie from My Brother's Editor for line edits.
Rosa from My Brother's Editor for proofreading.
Hang Le for the cover and branding for the entire series.
All the bloggers who read, review, share and/or promote us.
The Piper Rayne Unicorns in our Facebook group who are our biggest cheerleaders!
Every reader who took the time to read this book! Thank you for granting us your most precious resource—time. We don't take that lightly.

Make sure you check out Miles and Bryce's book, Something Like Hate, the first book in our Chicago Grizzlies series!

xo,
Piper & Rayne

about piper & rayne

Piper Rayne is a USA Today Bestselling Author duo who write "heartwarming humor with a side of sizzle" about families, whether that be blood or found. They both have e-readers full of one-clickable books, they're married to husbands who drive them to drink, and they're both chauffeurs to their kids. Most of all, they love hot heroes and quirky heroines who make them laugh, and they hope you do, too!

also by piper rayne

Kingsmen Football Stars

You Had Your Chance, Lee Burrows

You Can't Kiss the Nanny, Brady Banks

Over My Brother's Dead Body, Chase Andrews

Chicago Grizzlies

Something like Hate

Something like Lust

Something like Love

Lake Starlight

The Problem with Second Chances

The Issue with Bad Boy Roommates

The Trouble with Runaway Brides

The Modern Love World

Charmed by the Bartender

Hooked by the Boxer

Mad about the Banker

The Single Dad's Club

Real Deal

Dirty Talker

Sexy Beast

Hollywood Hearts

Mister Mom

Animal Attraction

Domestic Bliss

Bedroom Games

Cold as Ice

On Thin Ice

Break the Ice

Box Set

Charity Case

Manic Monday

Afternoon Delight

Happy Hour

Blue Collar Brothers

Flirting with Fire

Crushing on the Cop

Engaged to the EMT

White Collar Brothers

Sexy Filthy Boss

Dirty Flirty Enemy

Wild Steamy Hook-up

The Rooftop Crew

My Bestie's Ex

A Royal Mistake

The Rival Roomies

Our Star-Crossed Kiss

The Do-Over

A Co-Workers Crush

Made in United States
North Haven, CT
28 April 2023

35973302R00136